CONFESSIONS OF A SERIAL KISSER

Also by Wendelin Van Draanen

The Sammy Keyes Mysteries

Wendelin Van Draanen

CONFESSIONS OF A SERIAL KISSER

EMBER

Text copyright © 2008 by Wendelin Van Draanen Parsons
Cover art copyright © 2009 by Alexandra.mothersvea.se

Visit us on the Web! randomhouseteens.com

Educators and librarians, for a variety of teaching tools, visit us at RHTeachersLibrarians.com

The Library of Congress has cataloged the hardcover edition of this work as follows:
Van Draanen, Wendelin.
Confessions of a serial kisser / Wendelin Van Draanen.
p. cm.
Summary: After reading her mother's secret collection of romance novels during her parents' difficult separation, seventeen-year-old Evangeline Logan begins a quest for the perfect kiss.
ISBN 978-0-375-84248-1 (trade) — ISBN 978-0-375-94248-8 (lib. bdg.) —
ISBN 978-0-375-84992-3 (ebook)
[1. Kissing—Fiction. 2. Interpersonal relations—Fiction. 3. Best friends—Fiction.
4. Friendship—Fiction. 5. High schools—Fiction. 6. Schools—Fiction.
7. Family problems—Fiction.] I. Title.
PZ7.V2857Con 2008
[Fic]—dc22
2007049027

ISBN 978-0-375-84249-8 (tr. pbk.)

Printed in the United States of America
10 9 8 7 6 5 4 3

For fans of **FLIPPED**,
especially the ones who wrote me letters.

CONFESSIONS OF A SERIAL KISSER

1

Dirty Laundry

My name is Evangeline Bianca Logan, and I am a serial kisser.

I haven't always been a serial kisser. There was a time not that long ago when I had next to no kissing experience. It's interesting how things can change so fast—how you can go from being sixteen with very few lip-locking credentials to being barely seventeen and a certified serial kisser.

It all started one day with dirty laundry.

At least that's what *I* trace it back to.

My mother had said, "Evangeline, please. I could really use some help around the house." She'd looked so tired, and what with homework and the amount of time I'd been wasting at Groove Records looking through old LPs and CDs, I *had* been slacking. Especially compared to the hours she'd been working.

So after school the next day I kicked into gear. I had the condo to myself because Mom was working her usual eleven A.M. to eight P.M. shift, and since my taste in music is old blues and classic rock (probably thanks to being bombarded with it since my early days in the womb), I selected an Aerosmith greatest hits CD and cranked it up.

I made the kitchen spotless during "Mama Kin," "Dream On," "Same Old Song and Dance," and "Seasons of Wither," sang along with "Walk This Way" and "Sweet Emotion" while I cleaned the bathroom, then tidied the bedrooms through "Last Child" and "Back in the Saddle."

It was during the pulsing beat of "Dude (Looks Like a Lady)" that I began my fateful search for wayward laundry.

Laundry at the Logan girls' residence isn't found in hampers. It's found on the floor, draped over chairs, putrefying in boxes and baskets . . . it's anywhere my mom and I want to dump it. And in my rocked-out state I was checking for laundry in places I'd never looked before. Like on her closet floor, behind and between the big packing boxes that still serve as my mother's dresser, and then under my mother's bed. It was there that I discovered one dusty sock and a whole library of books.

Not just random books, either.

Romance books.

At first all I could do was gawk at the covers. I'd seen these kinds of books at the grocery store, but they were so obviously stupid and trashy that I wouldn't be caught dead actually looking at one.

But now here I was with a whole library of trash in front of me and no worries that someone might spot me.

So as strains of "Angel" began playing, I looked!

I checked out all the covers, then started reading the blurbs on the backs. Aerosmith eventually quit playing, but I didn't even notice. I was skimming pages, laughing at the ridiculous, flowery prose, my jaw literally dropping as I read (in great detail) how one book's chisel-chested man and his luscious lady "joined souls in sublime adoration."

I couldn't believe what I'd found. Couldn't believe my mother! While I was slogging through *The Last of the Mohicans* and *The Red Badge of Courage* for my insane literature teacher, Miss Ryder, my mother was reading books with bare-chested men and swooning women? Miss Ryder would have an English-lit fit over these books, and for once I'd agree with her!

But for each book I put down, I picked up another. And another. And another. Why, I don't know. Was I looking for more soul joining? I don't think so. Something to hold over my mother's head? She didn't need any more ravaging. I think it was more that I was still in shock over my mom being a closet romance freak.

But after ten pages out of the middle of a book called *A Crimson Kiss,* something weird happened: I actually kind of cared about Delilah, the woman that the story was about.

I read some more out of the middle, but since I didn't get why Delilah was in her predicament, I went back to the beginning to figure it out.

I have no idea where the time went. I was carried away by the story, swept into the swirl of romance, racing hearts, anticipation, and love. They were things that were missing in my real life. After six months of watching my parents' marriage implode, I found it hard to believe in true love.

But inside the pages of this book my parents' problems vanished. It was just Delilah and her hero, Grayson—a man whose kiss would save her from her heartache and make her feel *alive*.

Love felt possible.

One kiss—the right kiss—could conquer all!

So I read on, devouring the book until I was jolted back to reality by my mother jangling through the front door.

Busted!

In my panic, it didn't even occur to me that *she* was really the one busted. I just shoved her books back under her bed and escaped to my room with *A Crimson Kiss*.

2

Shifting Paradigms

OVER THE NEXT FEW MONTHS I read every book in my mother's sub-mattress library, including a self-help book on finding your inner power and another one titled *A Call to Action* on how to take charge of your life. (Books she'd gotten, no doubt, to help her get over my two-timing dad.)

But it was *A Crimson Kiss* that I kept going back to. It was *A Crimson Kiss* that I read and reread. The other romance novels didn't have any layers to them; no real *guts*. It was like pop versus rock. Some people like the pure tones of pop, but to me it's just gloss. There's nothing *behind* it. Give me the heart-wrenching gritty guts of blues or rock any day.

Not that *A Crimson Kiss* was written in a gritty way, but it sure was heart-wrenching. And the kissing was incredibly passionate! I dreamed scenes from it at night, waking some mornings still feeling the breathless transcendence of a perfectly delivered kiss.

Once I was fully awake, though, reality would strike.

It was just a dream.

Just a romantic fantasy.

Then one morning, I found a book on the kitchen table beside an empty bowl. (A bowl with telltale signs of midnight bingeing on chocolate ice cream.) The book was splayed open, spine up, and the title was *Welcome to a Better Life*.

I looked it over as I ate my usual before-school bowl of cereal (in this case, Cheerios). The section titles were things like: "Re-envision Your Life!"; "The Time Is NOW!"; "The Change Is Yours to Make!"; "Living Your Best Life!"; "See It, Be It!"; "What Are You Waiting For?"; "Shift Your Paradigm!"; and "Four Steps to Living Your Fantasy!"

Four steps to living my fantasy?

This I had to see.

Too many anecdotes and testimonials later, the author finally put forth step number one:

Define Your Fantasy.

Okaaaaay.

I poured myself a second bowl of Cheerios and defined my fantasy:

I wanted love. A love like Grayson and Delilah's.

But something about that felt wrong. It was too heavy. Too serious.

I took a bite of Cheerios, and as I munched, the image of Grayson kissing Delilah drifted through my mind.

That was it.

The kiss.

I wanted my own "crimson kiss."

I went back to the book and discovered that step number two was easy:

Speak Your Fantasy.

"I want a crimson kiss," I whispered into the quiet of the kitchen, feeling more than a little silly.

Step three: *See* Your Fantasy.

I closed my eyes and pictured myself as Delilah, pictured Grayson sweeping me into his arms, looking lovingly into my eyes, his mouth descending toward mine, his lips brushing against mine, warm and tender, full of smoldering passion. . . .

Oh, yeah. I could definitely see it.

I shook off the shivers, then turned the page and discovered that step number four was: Live Your Fantasy.

Live my fantasy?

How was I supposed to do that?

All the book really offered by way of explanation was, "See it, believe it, live it."

I snorted and slapped the book shut. What a rip-off!

Then I noticed the kitchen clock.

7:30?

Already?

I flew around the condo getting ready for school, and despite some unintentional banging and clanging, I managed to slip out the door without waking my mother.

I hurried toward school, and as I walked, my flip-flops seemed to slap to the rhythm of the steps outlined in *Welcome to a Better Life*.

Speak Your Fantasy.

See Your Fantasy.

Live Your Fantasy.

The cadence of it was catchy. Like the chorus of a song.

Speak Your Fantasy.

See Your Fantasy.

Live Your Fantasy.

And as it repeated in my head, I suddenly realized how much my life had been dominated by my parents' breakup. When was the last time I'd even thought about my own love life?

Speak Your Fantasy.

See Your Fantasy.

Live Your Fantasy.

Maybe it *could* be that easy. I could just live my own life! Get out from under their dark cloud! Have some *fun*.

Speak Your Fantasy.

"I want a crimson kiss!" I shouted into the sky.

See Your Fantasy.

I spun in a fantasy dance across an intersection, adored in my mind's eye by my own dashing Grayson.

Live Your Fantasy.

I hurried onto the Larkmont High School campus. My life was going to change!

3

Adrienne Willow

I MADE A BEELINE ACROSS THE QUAD—hurrying past the outdoor stage, zigzagging between cement lunch tables and across patchy grass— to reach my best friend, Adrienne Willow, who was perched on "our" brick planter, organizing her binder.

I hopped up beside her. "I had an epiphany this morning."

"Really?" she asked, snapping the rings of her binder closed. "What's that?"

"I'm done being dragged through the knothole of my parents' life. I'm going to start living my own."

She looked up, blinked, then whooped and jumped off the planter. "It's about time!"

"Do you know how much I've missed this year? I didn't go out for volleyball, I didn't join link crew or help with the warmth drive . . . all I've done is live under their dark cloud and *study*."

Adrienne had been bouncing with excitement, but she suddenly stopped, so I followed her line of sight across the quad.

It was Tatiana Phillips.

"It wasn't her fault," I said quietly. "It was her mom's. And my dad's. I shouldn't have let it stop me."

"From playing volleyball?" Adrienne asked, giving me her trademark squint. "No one could have played under those circumstances!" She snorted. "Her mother and your dad sitting together at games? Please."

I looked down. Adrienne has an uncanny way of putting her finger on the heart of the hurt.

The warning bell clanged. "The point is," I said firmly, "I'm through letting it ruin my life. I need to have some fun. I need to shift paradigms."

"You need to *what*?"

I laughed, then spread out my arms and looked down at my baggy John Lennon "Imagine" T-shirt and frayed jeans. "I need a makeover!" I caught her eye. "And I need you to help me."

She collected her things. "Anything," she said. "You know that. Anything."

Then she gave me a tight hug, and we hurried off to our first-period classes.

4

Robbie Marshall

FOR THE PAST COUPLE OF YEARS I've made a habit of ignoring Robbie Marshall. He's gorgeous, but that's exactly why I ignore him.

Like he needs one more girl fawning over him?

We used to be friendly, but that was back in middle school. Back when he wasn't afraid to be smart. Back before he grew into Robbie Marshall, gorgeous jock.

So in first period all the other girls in class paid attention to Robbie Marshall's biceps, and I paid attention to Mrs. Fieldman's math lesson. Mrs. Fieldman is a real pro. She's clear and concise, and there's no falling asleep in her class—she covers more material in a day than some teachers do in a week, and if you don't pay attention, you can kiss a good grade goodbye.

After math I continued through my morning classes, slipping into the typical rhythm of a school day. But somewhere in the middle of third period I realized that I was doing what I'd been doing all year: focusing, taking notes, getting a jump on the homework. Fun was no part of the equation. I was certainly not living my fantasy!

So as third period wound down, I did something I never do—I packed up early, and when the bell rang, I bolted out of the classroom.

Apparently I'm a complete klutz at bolting from classrooms, because not only did I hurt my wrist, I managed to slam the door into someone walking by.

Someone who turned out to be . . . Robbie Marshall.

"Sorry!" I said, turning beet red.

"No problem," he replied.

And then he smiled at me.

Diamonds seemed to dance between his lips as he gazed at me. His eyes twinkled smoky gray. His hair looked like it had been combed through with sunshine.

Then he was gone.

But just like that, my fantasy found a direction.

A *destination*.

I staggered to my fourth-period class, out of breath and (granted) out of my mind. Suddenly all I could see was Robbie Marshall's face.

All through Miss Ryder's American-lit lecture I fantasized about Robbie Marshall.

His eyes.

His smile.

His *lips*.

I didn't concentrate on my classwork, didn't scrutinize the red comments on the essay Miss Ryder passed back. By the end of class my chance collision with the school's most gorgeous jock was completely entwined with my newfound desire to live my fantasy.

It had all become perfectly clear.

I needed to kiss Robbie Marshall.

5

New Attitude

AT LUNCH WHEN I TOLD ADRIENNE WHAT I WANTED TO DO, she gave me her trademark squint and said, "Robbie *Marshall*? How in the world do you expect to kiss Robbie Marshall?"

"Shhh!" I yanked her off to our corner of the quad, checking around for gossipmongers. "Look. I've got assets—"

"Of course you do! But he just barely broke up with Sunshine, and in case you haven't noticed, she is *not* over him!" Adrienne whispered. "Plus Jasmine Hernandez wants him *bad,* and Nicole Bruma wants him *back.*"

"So?"

"So? *So?* Helloooo, Evangeline . . . you know I love you—you're witty and thoughtful and loyal and smart . . . and very pretty"—she leaned in—"but since when can you compete with Sunshine, Jasmine, *or* Nicole?"

I scowled at her. "Thanks for the vote of confidence."

"Evangeline, get real!" She squinted at me harder. "And why him?"

I shrugged. "He's gorgeous. And, well, experienced." I arched an eyebrow in her direction. "A crimson kiss does not reside on the lips of inexperience."

"A crimson kiss? What . . . from that book? You're still obsessed with that?"

I looked down and shrugged again. "I'm just trying to have some fun, okay? I'm trying to live a fantasy." I looked at her through my lashes. "You said you'd help me. You said 'Anything.' "

She bit her lip as she studied me, so I gave her a puppy-dog look and said, "Please?"

"Okay, okay," she laughed. "I'll help you. So what's the plan?"

I smiled, happy to have her in my corner. "I really do need a new look."

She eyed my clothes and nodded. "Have any idea what?"

"Something to match my new attitude."

"You're talking about clothes? Makeup? Hair?"

"The works. What are you doing after school today?"

Her forehead crinkled. "Today? I've got choir practice until five."

"Can you come over after?"

She hesitated, then said, "Sure. Why not?"

I hugged her. "You're the best!"

6

Ch-ch-ch-changes

AFTER I GOT HOME, I couldn't seem to concentrate on my school-work. I'd picked up a hair-highlighting kit at the pharmacy on my way home, so instead of studying math, I studied the directions. Then I studied myself in the mirror, trying to decide how much highlighting I really wanted to do. The old me would have gone subtle. The new me was saying, "Take chances! Make a *real* change!"

I moved on to studying my mom's wardrobe (which is way cooler than mine), trying to find something that spoke to me from her boxes of still-packed clothes.

Then I studied the clock. It was already five-thirty.

What was taking Adrienne so long?

The phone rang five minutes later, and when I picked up, Adrienne said, "I'm so sorry! Mom made lasagna and she insisted I come home. Can we do it tomorrow?"

I told her, "Sure," but after I hung up, I decided to dive in on my own. I'd been waiting all afternoon to make a change, and I didn't want to put it off any longer!

So I took out the scissors, cranked up some classic David Bowie, and started snipping.

I'm actually good at cutting hair, because I've butchered Adrienne's locks enough times to figure it out. I've also cut her brother Brody's hair, and now that I've got skills, my mom lets me trim hers, too. Cutting hair is just basically applied geometry ... which can get a little tricky when you're facing the mirror image of yourself, trying to get the scissors to go the right way.

I always do my own hair dry, which isn't the best, but I seem to be able to see what I'm doing better that way. And I usually just trim little bits, but now after a few timid snips, I let the spirit of Bowie's "Changes" take charge of the scissors.

I took a deep breath and started *cutting.*

All through "Suffragette City," "Ziggy Stardust," "The Jean Genie," and "Rebel Rebel" I cut in layers. I cut off length. I gave myself long side-swept bangs and a cute shaggy flip at the nape of the neck. It was a style that cried out for oversized hoop earrings, eyeliner, and go-go boots!

Ch-ch-ch-changes!

I felt good!

Mom called as I was mixing up the highlighter. "Evangeline, honey. Would you mind vacuuming the carpets tonight? I didn't get to it this morning, and they really need it." She sounded tired, like she always does, but this time I was feeling so good that it didn't bring me down.

"Sure," I said brightly. "Anything else?"

She hesitated, then said, "Thank you. I needed that. But no. Unless you want to wipe up that old orange juice spill in the fridge."

"Will do!"

I hung up and got busy streaking my hair.

Bowie sang "Ashes to Ashes," "Fashion," and "Under Pressure."

I shouted along.

And while the highlights timer ticked and radical chemicals bleached streaks into my hair, I vacuumed crumbs and fuzz and a month's worth of dust out of the carpet, singing along when "Let's Dance" came on.

My dad called as I was putting the vacuum cleaner away.

"How are you?" he asked.

And just like that I was back under the cloud.

I wanted to say, "Better than I've been in ages! I'm moving on, Dad. Moving on!" But what came out of my mouth is what always comes out of my mouth when my dad tries to engage me in conversation. "We're sorry, you've reached a number that has been disconnected. Please hang up and *don't* try again."

My highlights timer dinged as I hung up the phone.

So I cranked up "Dancing in the Street," then went to the sink to wash out my hair.

7

Emergence

ADRIENNE ABOUT FELL OVER when she saw me the next day. "Who did your hair? Whose jeans are those? I love the eyeliner! Wow, you look gorgeous!"

"I did it myself." I turned around for her. "How's the back?"

She fluffed my hair with her fingertips. "The back is fantastic! How did you *do* that?"

"I just went for it."

"No kidding!"

"You want me to do yours?"

"Wow." She pulled a scared little face. "Maybe . . . ?"

Resident jock Stu Dillard—also known as Studly—walked by, giving me a double take *and* an exaggerated once-over. "Evangeline!" He held a finger out toward me. "Tssss!"

I tried to be cool as I nodded an acknowledgment, but broke into giggles after he was gone.

"Stu Dillard just called you hot!" Adrienne whispered, her eyes enormous. She shook her head a little. "Wow. Wow, wow, wow."

"Well!" I said, trying to contain the complete bubble-up I was feeling inside. "We are off to a promising start!"

Unfortunately, during first-period math that promising start came to a grinding halt.

Robbie Marshall didn't notice anything different about me.

Correction.

He didn't notice me at all.

That might have been because he wasn't in the habit of noticing me, or, more likely, because it was Thursday.

Every girl on campus knows (as do the boys, but they wouldn't be caught dead admitting it) that on Tuesday and Thursday mornings Robbie Marshall's arms are glorious works of sculpted art.

It's not that they're not impressive during the rest of the week; it's just that every Tuesday and Thursday he does an insane morning workout that leaves his biceps bulging, his triceps ripped, and his forearms looking like superhero sledgehammers.

And since he hasn't cooled down from his workout yet, first-period math is the place to be if you want to admire Robbie Marshall's arms. Tank tops, muscle shirts, tight T's . . . he wears as little as he can get away with.

So maybe he didn't notice my new look because everyone was busy noticing him. Or maybe it was because he did his usual last-minute slide into his seat and Sandra Herrera (who sits between the two of us) was blocking his view.

Whatever the case, when Mrs. Fieldman commanded, "Pass your papers left!" I took Kenny Altemore's homework, handed mine to Sandra Herrera (which took a little patience, as Sandra was recovering from her near-physical contact with Robbie when she passed her homework to him), then got down to the business of math-class mechanics. By the time Mrs. Fieldman was through calling out answers, reviewing missed problems, and explaining the new section, I'd almost forgotten that there was anything different about me.

When the bell rang, Robbie was out of his seat and through the door before I'd even put away my binder.

"I like your new look," Lacey Egbert said as she passed by my desk.

"Thanks!" I said, sliding my binder inside my book bag.

Then all of a sudden Robbie was back. The cool air, it seemed, had alerted him to the fact that he'd forgotten his letterman jacket.

After years of ignoring him, I was now paying attention to nothing *but* him. He snatched his jacket off the back of his seat and was in the middle of putting it on when he noticed me.

He hesitated for maybe half a second, one arm in, one arm out. Then he smiled that gorgeous diamond-dusted smile at me as he swept his other arm through the sleeve of his jacket.

On cue, I smiled back.

Then I looped my book bag over my arm upside down, spilling everything inside it onto the floor.

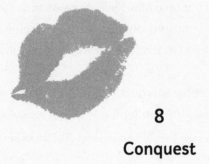

8

Conquest

FOR THE NEXT TWO WEEKS Adrienne helped me arrange "chance encounters" with Robbie Marshall. She'd scout him out in the Snack Shack line during break, slyly cut in a few people back, then call out, "Evangeline! Over here!" and wave for me to join her.

She interviewed him for the *Larkmont Times* (our illustrious school newspaper), and when I "happened" to saunter by, she pointed me out and casually mentioned that every guy in school seemed to be falling over me and my smashing new look.

She dragged me along as she boldly infiltrated his corner of the quad, delivering an early copy of the *Larkmont Times* for his perusal.

"Hey, Evangeline," he said to me, flashing diamond dust my way.

"Hey," I said back, then somehow stumbled on a dandelion.

Klutzy or not, I was definitely being noticed. But it all seemed to be taking so long! I was seeing my fantasy, and he was seeing me, but that was it for two long weeks. What was it going to take to go from seeing to living?

So Wednesday night I rummaged through my mother's boxes of clothes and discovered an outstanding Rolling Stones T-shirt. It was creamy pink with the trademark lips and tongue. It was soft and stretchy, with a scoop neck and cap sleeves—my favorite style.

Next, I raided her jewelry box and found a pair of oversized hoop earrings and half a dozen bangle bracelets.

On to her perfume! (Which was still packed in an old shoe box under the bathroom sink.) I sampled everything from Happy to White Diamonds and settled on a subtle, musky fragrance.

The last detail was makeup. I'd been wearing it pretty subtle, but it was time to go for a redder lipstick. A darker mascara. A wider, more dramatic flare of eyeliner.

I stashed everything in my closet, and the next morning I got decked out and slipped through the condo door ready to live my fantasy!

Robbie did his usual at-the-bell slide into his seat, and, it being a Thursday, girls all around ogled his bulging arms.

I, on the other hand, sharpened my pencil and took my time walking back to my seat, consciously avoiding Robbie (and any potential tripping hazards).

Mrs. Fieldman took roll, then commanded us to pass our homework to the person on our left. I accepted Kenny Altemore's homework, then turned to find Robbie Marshall staring at me.

Sandra Herrera was absent, leaving no human obstruction between me and Robbie. Fate, it seemed, was all for me living my fantasy.

♥ 23 ♥

For a moment we both held on to my homework and gazed into each other's eyes. He breathed out a heavy "Whoa," which made me blush and turn away. But I kept glancing over at him throughout the period, and I couldn't help noticing that he spent a lot more time stealing looks at me than watching Mrs. Fieldman work problems on the whiteboard.

When the bell rang, I made sure my book bag was right side up before looping it over my shoulder, then timed my exit to coincide with his. I smiled at him as we walked outside together, trying to look cool and confident, as my knees quivered me along.

"You look *good,*" he whispered.

"You think?" I countered, my heart racing. "How good?"

"*Real* good," he said.

We were a safe distance from the classroom, so I edged closer to him and smiled. "Kissably good?"

Before I could fully process that those words had really come out of *my* mouth, Robbie Marshall glanced around quickly, then swept a bionic arm around me and pulled me toward him.

The scene where Delilah is consumed by the magic of her first kiss with Grayson flashed through my mind. I watched Robbie's lips, willing them to meet mine.

My chin tipped up.

This was it!

My eyes eased closed.

I was living my fantasy!

My mouth pursed ever so slightly.

I was quivering all over—this was unbelievable!

And then Robbie *attacked.* I swear that brute almost chipped my tooth with his diamond-dusted teeth! And while I was reeling from the shock of *that,* he shoved his tongue halfway down my throat and nearly gagged me!

"Oh, yeah," he said, panting hard as he pulled away. "Oh, *yeah.*" Then he wiped his mouth with the back of his hand and rushed off.

9

Aftermath

ON MY WAY OVER TO SECOND PERIOD, I swished out my mouth at the water fountain. I felt slimed. Disgusted.

That kiss wasn't crimson!

It wasn't even pink!

I'm not sure it even *qualified* as a kiss.

It was more like mouth-to-mouth with a mackerel!

I was still reeling when I slipped into my second-period seat. Even on a good day it would have been hard to focus on Mr. Anderson's lecture on ancient Chinese dynasties (he's very much *not* one of those teachers who make history come alive). But after the mackerel-mouth incident it was impossible. My focus was on kissing.

Is that how Robbie had kissed Sunshine Holden?

And if it was, how did he ... do other stuff?

I shuddered and actually tried to focus on Mr. Anderson's

droning. ". . . but in the year 960 a new power, Song, reunified most of China proper. The Song period divides into two phases due to the forced abandonment of north China in 1127 by the Song court, which was unable to push back the nomadic invaders. . . ."

My mind wandered off.

Did all guys kiss like that?

Were Delilah and Grayson *purely* fictional?

Was I swimming in a sea of mackerels?

Sharks?

Barracudas?

What did I want?

Guppies?

"Miss Logan?"

I snapped to. "Huh?"

"Your attention should be directed up here."

So I directed my attention up there, but focusing on his lecture was hopeless. Instead, I started thinking that Mr. Anderson's having five children was an absolute miracle. The man has no lips (to speak of), no hair (worth mentioning), and no level of hotness (whatsoever)! How'd he ever get close enough to a woman to spawn five children?

When second period was finally over, I escaped the classroom, desperate to find Adrienne. I was dying to tell her about Robbie Marshall!

But in the high seas of secondary education, the undertow of gossip is incredibly fast and strong. Adrienne already knew.

"Is it true?" she gasped when she saw me. "Did he really kiss you?"

I nodded and pulled a face. "Yes, and it was disgusting!"

"What? Disgusting? How can that be?" She squinted at me. "I demand details!"

But over her shoulder I could see that the details would have to wait.

Sunshine Holden was storming across the quad.

Straight for me.

10

Sunshine on My Shoulder

"*What* do you think you're *doing*?" Sunshine demanded.

"Uh . . . having break?"

She shoved my shoulder. "Bitch."

"Hey!" Adrienne shouted, dumping her backpack and stepping forward.

"Take it easy, Sunshine," I said. "Everything's cool."

"No, it's not! How dare you kiss my boyfriend?"

"Your boyfriend?" Adrienne asked, holding her ground. "What are you talking about? You guys broke up weeks ago!"

"Yeah? Well, as of last night we're back together!"

Adrienne and I both eyed each other with little Oooohs. Then Adrienne said, "Uh . . . maybe you should take this up with Robbie?" She cocked her head in my direction. "Obviously she didn't know."

Sunshine ignored Adrienne and shoved me again. "What made you think you could just go up and *kiss* him? You have a reputation for being smart, but that was really *dumb*."

I opted not to comment on *her* reputation. "Uh . . . it didn't exactly happen that way, Sunshine." I took a step back. "But I'm not after Robbie, okay?"

"Oh, right! Like I haven't noticed the way you've been circulating him?"

Circulating him?

I let it slide. "Look. I have no intention of coming between you guys. He's all yours."

"Damn straight!" she said. "And if I ever catch you anywhere *near* him, you'll be so dead!"

The warning bell put an end to our jolly conversation. Sunshine stormed off, and Adrienne let out a low whistle. "Wow! That was intense!"

It had been. Sunshine had always acted so aloof. So *superior*. I hadn't thought of her as the catfight type, but she had certainly shown some claw. I shook my head. "That was one dangerous kiss. And I don't mean that in a good way!"

Adrienne grabbed her things and started backpedaling away from me. "I can't be late to class, and I've got a choir meeting at lunch. But I'm actually free after school. Can you come over? You just have to! I don't even know what happened!"

"Sure."

"Meet me at Brody's truck!" she called.

"See you there!" I called back, then waved and ran off to third period.

11

Willow Talk

ADRIENNE AND I BOTH HAVE OUR LICENSE, we just don't get to drive much. My mom and I have opposite schedules and she always has the car, which makes sense because it's her car. My dad promised to buy me my own car when I turned sixteen, but as it turns out, he's a pathological liar. And Adrienne's parents rely on Adrienne's brother, Brody (who has his own truck), to do the shuttling.

Brody's one of those work-hard-and-save-your-money kind of guys who won't buy a Coke out of a machine because he thinks it's a rip-off. Then he goes broke dropping his whole wad on something big like a truck and has to start saving all over again.

My philosophy is spend-as-you-go. Buy the Coke. Enjoy every day.

Of course, I don't have a car.

Adrienne and I call Brody's truck the Chevy, because it's wide and slightly lowered and ripe-tomato red. It's a vintage GMC, but we still call it the Chevy, which drives him crazy, and I do so love driving Brody Willow crazy! He's like the big brother my parents forgot to provide. In addition to being a responsible saver, he's the quintessential student, and unlike me, he seems to find getting A's easy. He thinks physics is fascinating and has never had a B.

He's also never had a girlfriend; has never gone on a *date* (even though Adrienne and I have tried like mad to set him up). I don't think he's gay, but I wouldn't care if he was.

"Hey, Bro!" I said when I spotted him in the parking lot. "Wassup!"

"Get in," he said, rolling his eyes.

I scooted across the worn vinyl bench seat to my usual in-the-middle spot, and Adrienne came flying in right behind me. "Home, James!" she commanded. Then she grabbed my arm and whispered, "The gossip is insane!"

"I haven't heard anything," I said quite innocently as I turned on the radio and tuned in my favorite station.

As Neil Young's "Like a Hurricane" blasted from the speakers, Brody pulled into the traffic jam of students trying to escape the joys of secondary education. "I haven't either," he said.

Adrienne reached over and changed the radio station, muttering, "What *is* this song?" but Brody stopped her, saying, "At least give it a chance!"

"Yeah, choirgirl," I laughed. "Give it a chance!"

Adrienne rolled her eyes, then put Brody on the spot, saying, "So, you haven't said anything about Evangeline's new look."

"Huh?" He was busy with traffic, but he managed to glance at me. "She looks nice."

Fashion isn't exactly a priority for Brody. He and Adrienne both get a clothing allowance, but he never seems to buy anything new. He just cycles through the same old T-shirts. Still, I couldn't let *nice* stand. "Don't be fooled, Bro! I'm mean as mercury!"

I don't know why I said mercury, but Brody thought it was the funniest thing he'd ever heard. He chuckled about it the whole way home. Maybe in the cultish world of advanced placement physics, mercury is known as an evil substance, I don't know.

When Adrienne and I were safely alone in her bedroom, she threw her backpack down, plopped in her desk chair, and said, "I want to hear every detail! Tell me what happened with Robbie!"

So I did. And when I described the "kiss," her face contorted into knots of revulsion. "Eeeeew."

"Exactly."

"Wow," she said after a minute. "How disappointing." Then after another moment of absorbing the shock of it all, she nodded at my Rolling Stones shirt. "Maybe that gave him the wrong idea?"

I looked down at the oversized lips and tongue. "A guy doesn't base his kisses on the T-shirt a girl's wearing! He's just a horrible kisser."

She shook her head. "So disappointing." Then she brightened. "But, Evangeline, think about it! You did it! Robbie Marshall *kissed* you! It's, like, *insane*."

"He mauled me," I grumbled, but she was right—it was a little surreal. I laughed. "Good thing it was a disaster, or I'd be in serious trouble!"

"Because of Sunshine?"

"Oh, yeah."

She laughed, too, then asked, "So now what?"

I lay back on her bed. "I'm not sure." I hugged a pillow as I propped myself up on an elbow. "How do you know if a guy's going to deliver a crimson kiss?"

She frowned. "All right, enough of this. What exactly *is* a crimson kiss?"

I smirked at her. "If you'd read the book, you'd understand."

She gave a little snort and rolled her eyes.

"See? You always put it down, but believe me, you want a crimson kiss too."

She studied me a moment, then said, "Fine. I'll read it."

I sat up. "Really?"

"Mm-hmm."

I snatched up my book bag and unzipped the small front pouch.

"You carry it with you? *Still?*"

I smiled and handed it over. The pages were curled, the cover tattered. "Be careful with it."

She sniggered. "Right."

"I'm serious."

She laughed. "You're insane!"

I laughed, too, and it felt good. I had a friend who cared, and (awful or not) I'd been kissed by the hottest guy at Larkmont High.

Maybe I wasn't living my fantasy *exactly,* but at least it felt like living.

12

The Kissing Corridor

I SHOULDN'T HAVE WORRIED about the awkwardness of seeing Robbie the next morning.

That boy totally ignored me.

Sunshine was waiting for him outside first period and made a big show of latching on to him as she escorted him away.

So it was true! Robbie had engaged in a little unauthorized mouth-to-mouth.

Tsk, tsk, tsk!

Such a naughty boy.

Since I was totally over him and his deceptive good looks, the news didn't even faze me. If Sunshine could resuscitate their relationship, more power to her.

But Adrienne's "So now what?" was a good question. Did I really want to go through weeks of pursuit again? And who would I pursue? Someone on campus had to be in possession of a crimson kiss, but who?

How could you tell?

At break Adrienne reported that she'd barely started reading the book, so that was no help. And since she was tied up with school-newspaper duties during lunch (leaving me to fend for myself in the quad with a still-angry Sunshine within striking distance), I wandered around thinking about kissing.

Obviously extreme hotness was no guarantee.

Maybe the place, the *setting*, was a factor. I took stock of my own setting and suddenly realized that I was *surrounded* by couples kissing. Against the buildings, on benches, under a tree . . . one, two, three, four, *five* couples kissing!

What was this?

The kissing corridor?

Justin Rodriguez was shuffling my direction, flanked by his friends Blaine York and Travis Ung. Justin had been in my sophomore biology class, but all I really knew about him was that he'd spent the year pining away for Lolita Rey.

He was obviously over that, because (despite his sorta geeky friends crimping his style) he had a confident swagger. "Hey," he said with a crooked grin.

"Hey," I said back. And as he swaggered by, we sort of locked eyes and smiled at each other. That was it. No polite long-time-no-see conversation, no clever repartee, just "Hey" and the locking of eyes. And as I exited the kissing corridor, I found myself thinking, *Nice. . . .*

Nice eyes.

Nice smile.

Nice hair.

Nice mouth.

Just *nice . . .*

During fifth-period chemistry I was still considering Justin Rodriguez's niceness. He *was* really cute. And maybe he was a romantic! He *had* pined away for Lolita Rey. Most guys don't show their vulnerable side, but he hadn't been able to hide it.

Yes, I decided, with his good looks and the right setting, Justin Rodriguez could very well be a crimson kisser!

I was brought back to the fascinating world of covalent bonding by Roper Harding's tap on my shoulder. "Do you get what he's talking about?" he whispered, eyeing the chalkboard where Mr. Kiraly had scrawled a series of complex molecular diagrams.

I tuned in to our teacher's heavy Hungarian accent and watched as he pointed to various parts of the diagram with his middle finger. (The middle finger may be used for pointing in Hungary, but someone should point out to *him* that an upended middle finger has an entirely different purpose in America.)

"No," I whispered over my shoulder.

"Yes, you do!" he said.

"Shh!" I whispered back.

I try to be kind to Roper Harding, but it's not easy. He's zitty, he's whiny, he's always borrowing paper, and he stinks. You haven't experienced full-throttle B.O. until you've sat near Roper Harding. Honestly, he smells four days dead.

"I know you get it. You've got an A in here!" he whispered.

"Shhh!" I whispered back, then leaned forward in my seat, wishing it was not just light but also *smell* that was reduced in strength by the square of the distance.

And then, to escape the smell of Roper Harding and the chalk-covered birdie-flipping finger of Mr. Kiraly, I returned to thoughts of Justin Rodriguez, wondering how I could set the scene to kiss him.

13

Groovy, Baby

ON MY WALK HOME FROM SCHOOL, I took a little detour to Groove Records. It's one of my dad's favorite hangouts, too, but going there after school is safe, because he's tied up with his day job doing network installations for the phone company.

Talk about making history come alive. Groove Records is like the world's coolest museum. There's not one new thing in the whole place. The walls are covered in old concert T-shirts and framed album covers, there are signed posters and collector guitars in glass cases, there are beads between rooms (and there are a *lot* of funky little rooms), and there's rock 'n' roll kitsch everywhere. I think I'm in love with the sheer funkiness of the place. The floors are creaky and slanted, and there are bottomed-out couches where you're welcome to park yourself all day and read ancient issues of *Rolling Stone*.

"Hey there, Bubbles!" the owner called over Black Sabbath's "Electric Funeral" when I jingled through the door. To him I've been

"Bubbles" since my dad introduced us when I was a baby. Apparently I had a major talent for blowing spit bubbles.

"Hey, Izzy," I called back. With his frizzy gray hair and beard, and his round, blue-tinted glasses, Izzy looks like one of the Jerry Garcia bobble-head dolls he has on the shelf behind the register.

"Saw your old man at the Bluez Barn last weekend. His band was smokin' hot, as usual."

"Izzy . . . ," I warned him. "We've discussed this. . . . You need to keep that sort of information to yourself."

He came out from behind the counter, making his way past long wooden crates of LPs and bins of trade-in CDs. "I . . . I just miss the old days."

I looked around his shop and chuckled, trying to lighten the mood. "No kidding."

"No, I mean you and him."

"Stop it," I said firmly. "This is my favorite place to be, but I can't come here anymore if you're going to keep bringing him up."

"I hear ya, I hear ya," he said quickly, but then brought him up again. "He hasn't been in in ages." He flipped through some LPs, shuffling a few that were out of order. "He's probably buying online now, huh?"

"I don't know! I don't care!" I almost stormed out, but then an odd connection gripped me. After shopping at Groove Records for nearly twenty years, my father probably *had* started shopping elsewhere.

Just like he'd done after close to twenty years of marriage.

Suddenly my heart went out to Izzy, and I reached for his arm. "I'm sorry."

He nodded. "You just gotta wonder why."

I snorted softly. "Exactly."

14

Chicken Soup for the Shattered Soul

I spent about an hour at Izzy's and on my way home decided to swing by Murphy's Market to see my mom. I actually like my mom quite a lot. And I missed her. The old her. The cheerful her. The pre-separation her.

And as I was walking along, I got the brilliant idea that maybe *she* was ready for a makeover, too! I knew just how I wanted to do her hair—long layers, red highlights . . . with chandelier earrings? Whoa. It would give her a whole new lease on life! Maybe over the weekend we could even do things together like we used to. Maybe *she* was finally ready to get out and have some fun, too!

So I breezed into Murphy's, anxious to see her. But after making the rounds at the checkout stands and not finding her, I walked up to the manager and said, "Hey, Mr. Banks, is my mom on break?"

He looked up from some paperwork he was reviewing at his little manager's stand by the value sacks of dog food. "Evangeline?" he asked. "My, haven't you grown up."

I suddenly felt very self-conscious. I'd forgotten that I'd changed my look. "Uh, yeah. It happens."

He laughed. "I'm sorry. I used to hate it when people said that kind of thing to me."

That threw me again, because I couldn't imagine it. Mr. Banks is a rosy-cheeked roly-poly puppy of a man. One of those belt-around-the-equator people. How had *he* looked as a teenager?

"But you were asking about your mother," he said with a warm smile. "I'm sorry to report that she called in sick. She sounded terrible." He went back to sifting through papers. "Tell her to take it easy and get well soon, will you?"

"Sure," I answered. And since I didn't know if she had a cold or the flu or just needed a day of R&R, I bought a couple of cans of chicken noodle soup, some Jell-O, and Gatorade, and hurried home.

I found her in bed, a box of Kleenex on one side, a pile of used tissues on the other. "Evangeline, honey!" she said, sounding very stuffy-nosed. "I'm so glad you're home. Come here." She grabbed a tissue and patted the bed. "How are you? Tell me all about yourself. It feels like ages since we talked."

"I'm fine. But I found out from Mr. Banks that you're not, so I picked up some chicken soup and Jell-O and—"

"You're wearing makeup?" she asked. "Since when have you been wearing makeup?"

"Mom, I'm a junior! Most girls have been wearing makeup since seventh grade."

"But you don't need makeup. You're a natural beauty." She cocked her head. "What made you decide to start wearing it?"

I shrugged. "I don't know. Just felt like making a change."

She studied me a moment. "I do like your hair. . . . I told you that already, right?"

She had. Sort of. It had been a cry of shock as I was moving from the bathroom to bed.

I smiled. "Actually, I was thinking that I could do yours."

She shook her head. "Oh, I don't think so."

"It might give you a lift, Mom." I set the groceries on the bed. "And it would be fun." I pointed out her earrings, dangling from my lobes. "I'd even lend you your earrings."

She sighed. "They look great on you, Evangeline."

"You don't mind?"

"Mind?" Her eyes suddenly brimmed with tears. "You brought me chicken soup and Jell-O. Borrow whatever you want." She wiped away a tear. "And yes. I would love some soup."

While I was heating it and unearthing the saltines, she called, "Do you and Adrienne have plans tonight?"

"She had choir practice after school today," I called back. "We talked about getting together"—I stuck my head back in her room— "but I think I'll just hang out with you."

"I miss you, too," she said, but it seemed to be too much effort for her to smile.

After I delivered the soup, I sat down on the edge of her bed and watched her eat. She looked so small. So vulnerable. My mind flashed to the countless times she'd sat on the edge of *my* bed feeding *me* soup, keeping me company, watching me.

Had she thought the same things?

Please feel better.

Get well.

And please, please . . . smile for me.

15

Coffee, Tea, or Me

THE NEXT MORNING my mom was feeling a little better and jonesing for some Starbucks chai. When I offered to run out and get the tea for her, she handed me a twenty and the car keys. "You really are an angel. And get whatever you want."

It felt great to be behind the wheel again. I powered down the windows, cranked up the radio, and enjoyed every second of the ride. It was a blast of total feel-good.

The Starbucks line was insane. Not that that's anything new. Especially midmorning on a Saturday. I'd be a frappuccino freak like half the school if it weren't for the line. Thank God for the line. Like I need a five-dollar-a-day addiction?

I'd applied a little makeup before leaving the house. After two weeks with it, I thought I looked washed out without it.

It was a good thing I had.

There were hotties all over the place!

Starbucks hotties come in a wide variety, but the two main categories are the rebel hotties and the fast-track hotties. Rebel hotties put a lock on you with their eyes but don't say much. I try to act cool and nonchalant when that happens, but I usually bump into something or miss the trash with my straw wrapper.

Rebel hotties bring out the dweeb in me.

Fast-track hotties, on the other hand, are usually a little older (like mid-twenties), but they smell good and look good, and they've obviously got something going on besides hanging around a coffee shop all day (unlike rebel hotties). They also don't mind engaging in clever conversation with others in the line.

Fast-track hotties make me feel older and more clever than I actually am.

Usually I see someone I recognize from school at Starbucks. Not this morning. This morning it was just me and the hotties. (And lots of moms, moms being big into Starbucks.)

Ahead of me was a fast-track hottie.

Behind me a couple of moms, comparing day-care notes.

In the chairs to my side Johnny-wanna-be-Depp and his java mates, getting an early start on their ne'er-do-welling.

Johnny locked on with his eyes, giving me a smirk and a twitch of the eyebrow.

I tried a cool smirk and a twitch in reply (although it probably looked more like I had a cramp), then moved forward in the line.

Unfortunately, the line hadn't actually moved, so I stepped on the heel of the fast-track hottie in front of me.

"Oh!" I said when he turned around. "I'm sorry!"

"No problem," he said with a smile. "Triple shot of molasses with your line this morning?"

I laughed. Our baristas are always pushing the flavor shots, which would be annoying if they weren't so cheery about it. But then I choked back a gasp as I took in this hottie's face. He had a cleft chin, a dimple in his left cheek, and beneath his long black lashes were dark, smoldering eyes.

Except for his clothes, he fit to a T the description of Grayson Manning in *A Crimson Kiss*.

I tried not to gape as he kept the conversation going. I tried to banter back, but all my clever replies seemed to form too late, backing up in my brain as we moved forward in line.

He ordered a double latte, and I watched him doctor it up at the sugar station as my order was being filled. Forget Justin Rodriguez—this was fate! I'd never, ever seen a guy with a cleft chin *and* a dimple in his cheek. There must be a reason he'd been in line right in front of me. There must be a reason he'd been so charming. There must be a reason I'd stepped on him!

The reason was destiny.

He was a crimson kisser!

He was also walking out the door.

No wave goodbye, no smile, no wink . . . he was just *leaving*.

But then I saw that he'd left his sunglasses on the sugar station counter.

"Evangeline!" the java goddess who'd filled my order called.

I snatched my tea, grabbed his sunglasses, and bolted out the door.

I looked around frantically.

Where had he gone?

There! Across the parking lot!

I ran over and inserted myself between him and his car.

"Oh, hi," he said, taking a step back.

"You forgot your sunglasses!" I panted.

"Hey, thank you."

His smile was like the morning sun breaking over the horizon. My knees went wobbly as I gazed into his beautiful eyes. And as I melted toward him, I gasped, "You also forgot to kiss me."

"Pardon me?"

"Kiss me," I whispered, and this time I grabbed his shirt and pulled him toward me.

16

Bulldozer

I'D LIKE TO REPORT that the earth moved when our lips met, but unfortunately it did not. *I* did, though. The guy was a bulldozer! His mouth pushed me back against his car until I was leaning way back and *sideways,* with my cup of tea reaching for the sky.

"Whoa!" I mumbled, then shoved him back with my free hand and ducked clear. "Uh...well...uh...thanks," I said, and escaped to my car.

I sat behind the wheel for a minute feeling breathless—in a run-for-your-life sort of way, not a fantasy-kiss kind of way.

How disappointing!

What a complete waste of a perfectly dimpled face!

On the drive home I tried to figure out what had gone so wrong. Robbie Marshall *should* have been a crimson kiss. The Starbucks guy *should* have been a crimson kiss.

Why weren't they?

There'd certainly been pre-kiss chemistry, but instead of worlds igniting, everything had just fizzled. How had I managed to pick a tongue thruster and a bulldozer?

Was it me?

Was *I* the horrible kisser?

Reading about kissing was obviously not the same thing as actually kissing!

I mulled it over for a few blocks, then started laughing out loud as the reality of what I'd done sank in.

I'd said, "Kiss me!" to a perfect stranger.

It was insane!

So impulsive!

So unlike me.

And yet, thinking about it made me feel . . . good.

Giddy.

Adrienne was going to *die*.

Mom was still in bed when I got home. And since I was still feeling giddy and strangely uninhibited, I delivered the tea and got next to her on the bed. "Tell me about your first kiss."

"My first kiss?" She sipped from the cup and said, "Ah, this is heavenly!" Finally she looked at me and asked, "Is there something I should know about? Some*one* I should know about? Is that why you're asking?"

I laughed. "No. I just want to hear about your first kiss. And I want to know if you've ever had a crimson kiss."

"A crimson kiss?" she asked, and I could see her trying to remember why the phrase was familiar. Suddenly her eyes got big and her mouth made a silent "Ohhhh" as she realized she was busted.

I grinned at her. "One of the hazards of having me clean house."

"I am so embarrassed."

I laughed. "Don't be. I actually liked that one." Then I asked, "So when did you start reading romance novels, anyway?"

"Kate Larson gave them to me—she thought it would get my mind off of . . . things."

"Did it?"

She shrugged. "More the opposite."

I didn't want to go down that dark, dank trail of despair, so I said, "Forget about the books. I want to hear about your first kiss, and any crimson kisses."

She took another sip of tea and said, "My first kiss was from your dad, and I would say that, yes, he's delivered more than a few crimson kisses."

"*Dad* was your first kiss?" I sat up straighter. "Wait. Does that mean you haven't kissed anyone *but* him?"

She nodded. "That's right."

"Your whole *life*?"

She shrugged. "My whole life."

I stared at her in disbelief. I knew they'd been high school sweethearts, but . . . I'd already kissed more guys than my mother?

I hadn't thought I could be any madder at my father, but now I was. She'd never even *kissed* another man, and he'd totally betrayed her!

My mother needed help.

Something had to change.

I took away her tea. "Get up," I said. "I'm giving you a makeover."

17

Cheap Trick

I LISTENED ATTENTIVELY to what Mom thought she wanted done, which boiled down to "A trim and *very* subtle highlights." Then I zipped off to the store and bought supplies for what *I* wanted done—a rich chestnut dye and ravishing red highlights.

When I returned, I found her reading *Welcome to a Better Life.* "Exactly!" I told her. "You need to live your fantasy!"

"You've read this, too?"

I nodded. "Speak your fantasy, see your fantasy, *live your fantasy.*"

She sighed. "My problem is I don't know what my fantasy should be."

I smiled at her. "Well, get ready. This makeover will change all that!"

I started by applying the chestnut dye. And when that process was done, I wrapped her shoulders with a towel, combed out her wet hair, and asked, "So what do you want to hear?"

She knew I was talking about music. "Cheap Trick," she said after a short consideration.

I decided not to comment on the irony of the band's name where my dad (or her haircut) was concerned. I just cranked up the CD and got busy snipping, not letting on that "subtle" was not part of my master plan.

"I Want You to Want Me" shook the walls. We had a little shout-along as I snipped and clipped and shaped up the back of her hair. Mom seemed to forget about what I was doing as the band powered through "Ain't That a Shame," "Surrender," and "If You Want My Love." By the time we'd made it through "I Can't Take It" and "Walk Away," she had sexy-long bangs and some razor-cut layers.

"You are looking amazing!" I said, very pleased with my handi-work.

She wanted a mirror.

"Forget it!" I told her, then blew out her hair. And when it was dry and I could see where streaks of ravishing red would look the best, I got busy on the final phase of my evil plan.

Cheap Trick was done playing and I was mixing up highlights, contemplating what CD I should put on next, when the phone rang.

"Hello?" I said, cradling the phone against my shoulder.

"Evangeline? This is your dad. Please don't hang up. I—"

"We're sorry, you've reached a number that has been disconnected. Please hang up and *don't* try again."

My mom sighed after I clicked off. "That's getting pretty old, sweetheart."

"His *calling* here's getting old! What's up with that? Why can't he just leave us alone?"

Very quietly, she said, "He and Janelle have split up."

"What?" I moved around to face her. "So she got tired of him and now he wants to be 'dad' again?"

"*He* broke it off. Quite a while ago."

My whole body felt flushed. The tops of my hands, my cheeks, my rib cage . . . everything suddenly felt hot. "Well, lucky Janelle." I cocked my head. "And how do you know all this?"

She was quiet a moment, then said, "We've met for coffee a few times."

"*What?*" But then I shook my head. "Never mind. I don't want to know." I wagged a finger at her. "When I'm done with you, you won't have time to have coffee with that two-timer! Men are going to be pounding down the door!"

I dug up The Who's greatest hits CD.

"Won't Get Fooled Again" seemed very appropriate.

18

Ravishing Red

I WAS IN THE MIDDLE of giving my mom's hair a final rinse at the sink when the phone rang again. Fortunately, it was Adrienne, not my dad.

"Hey," I said, holding the phone with one dripping hand while I sprayed my mom's head down with the other, "can I call you back? I'm rinsing out my mom. I gave her a radical cut and color."

"Radical?" my mom asked, banging her head on the faucet as she tried to pop up.

I pushed her back down, and into the phone I said, "Uh, I mean hot. She's gonna look hot."

My mother was not convinced. She bobbed up again, saying, "Is that why you won't let me see a mirror? What have you done? I trusted you!"

Before I could answer, Adrienne asked, "Did you really kiss a guy at Starbucks this morning?"

I pushed my mom down again and said, "Quit it, Mom! You're going to love it. Now let me finish rinsing!" And then into the phone I gasped, "Where'd you hear that?"

"Penelope Rozzwell, of all people. She heard it from Mary Blythe, who heard it from who-knows-who. So you're saying it's true?"

Mom was bobbing up again. "Just let *me* do it!"

"I'll call you back!" I said to Adrienne, and clicked off.

It was a real challenge keeping my mother away from a mirror. But I managed to blow her dry, style her, and apply a little makeup without letting her have a peek.

Finally I dug a pair of chandelier earrings out of her jewelry box, and after she'd slipped them in, I handed over a mirror.

She gasped when she saw herself.

She covered her mouth.

She turned side to side, touching the red highlights.

"Oh!" she said, sweeping aside the bangs, fluffing the layers. "Oh, wow!"

"Exactly," I said, feeling very proud of the transformation. "Everywhere you go, that's exactly what people are going to say. Oh, wow!"

She looked at me with glistening eyes and that all too familiar I'm-about-to-cry wrinkle pattern on her face.

So much for the makeup—it was about to get washed away.

But then something strange happened.

She blinked back the tears and *giggled*.

"It doesn't even look like me!" she gasped.

"Yes, it does. It looks like a refreshed you. A new you. But still you."

She gave me a hug, then looked at herself in the mirror again. "Oh, thank you, angel. Thank you!"

Then she turned to me, and there it was.

Her glorious, glowing smile.

19

Visitors

I GUESS I TOOK TOO LONG TO CALL ADRIENNE BACK, because around three o'clock the doorbell rang, and there she was.

"You can't avoid me," she said, pushing past me. "Best friends are not to be avoided."

"I wasn't avoiding you! I've been really busy with—"

Then she saw my mom. "Lorena?"

My mom had always asked Adrienne to call her Lorena, but this was the first time it didn't seem weird.

Maybe because it was the first time in a long time my mom didn't look like a mom. She'd put on some flattering jeans and a flowing olive green cami and she looked *hot*.

Adrienne gaped at me. "Wow, you *have* been busy!" She made my mother turn around. "That hairstyle is outstanding!"

"You're next," I said. "I'm on a roll!"

"I don't know. . . ." She shook her head and focused on my mom. "Wow! Wow, wow, wow!"

My mom seemed stoked. And after a dose of DayQuil, she didn't even sound sick. "You girls want to go to a movie? Out to an early dinner? Shopping?"

I laughed. "How about all three?"

But then the doorbell rang again, and when I answered it, I found myself face to face with my dad.

I hadn't seen him in months, but he looked exactly the same. His hair was stylishly scruffy; his mustache was trimmed neatly off his lip, swooping around into little "boots" beneath the corners of his mouth. He looked relaxed, but more dressed up than usual in fitted jeans and a sports coat.

"What about 'we don't want to talk to you' don't you understand?" I asked.

"Evangeline, please. I was a jackass and I know it. But I don't really want to discuss it on the stoop. Can I please come in?"

"I think you've summed it up nicely," I said back. "And there's really nothing to discuss, so please go away!"

I started to close the door, but he stuck a boot in and called, "Lorena?" into the condo.

Suddenly my mother appeared, a purse on her shoulder, her keys in hand. "I'm sorry, Jon. Whatever it is will have to wait. The girls and I were going out."

Before he could fully process her hot new look, she'd locked the door and breezed out to the sidewalk, pulling Adrienne and me along with her.

"Lorena, wait!" he called after her.

For once, she didn't listen.

20

Biology Experiment

ADRIENNE WAS FASCINATED by my Starbucks encounter. Not that I mentioned it in front of my mom—I had to slip it in piecemeal as we tooled around town eating and shopping. But by the time we were at The Bargain Boutique, waiting as my mother tried on yet another outfit, Adrienne was fully informed and liked the idea of trying to land Justin Rodriguez. "He's a much better choice than some random guy at a Starbucks!" she whispered. "And a romantic setting is a great idea. Delilah and Grayson were by the lake with swans and weeping willows and twittering birds."

"You read it!" I said.

"Well, most of it." She gave me a mild version of her trademark squint. "And I get it about the kissing, but Evangeline, really, it's not that great a book."

"It is too!"

She shook her head. "You're projecting something into it." Then she *really* squinted. "And I hate that Elise dies! Why does Elise have to die? No eight-year-old should have to die, fictional or otherwise!"

"But that's what drew Grayson and Delilah together."

"It's so manipulative. I hate books like that."

I crossed my arms. "So you hate my favorite book."

"No, I don't *hate* it. And the romance scenes *are* really great. I'll finish it and get it back to you on Monday, okay?" She grinned. "You're probably going through withdrawal, huh?"

It was kind of true.

She gave a knowing nod and said, "But back to the real world. I think Justin Rodriguez is a good prospect. He's actually sorta dashing-looking, and you're right—he seems like a romantic. He might actually be worthy of you!"

So with Adrienne's blessing I started mulling over ways and places to meet up with Justin Rodriguez, and by Monday I'd come up with the perfect setting.

The Prager Park gazebo.

It was a lovely gazebo—white, with elaborate scrollwork near the roof and trumpet vines climbing the latticework—and it was nestled among flowering magnolias and honeysuckle shrubs on a little grassy knoll.

Unfortunately, it was also near the basketball courts and a parking lot, but being there in the moonlight would be as close to a lake with swans and weeping willows as I'd be able to find.

The trouble was getting Justin there. Or, actually, finding him at all. I looked everywhere for him Monday morning, scoured the campus at break, kept an eagle eye out for him between classes . . . he was nowhere.

How was I supposed have a romantic rendezvous with a guy I couldn't find?

Once again Adrienne came to my rescue. She ran up to me in the quad during lunch and panted, "I tailed him to Room Five Twelve. He's eating lunch in there with Blaine York and Travis Ung!"

"In Mr. Webber's room?"

She shifted her backpack and nodded.

No wonder I couldn't find him. Mr. Webber might be nice, but nobody in their right mind would eat lunch in the bio lab. The walls ooze death and dissection, the air stinks, and after finishing biology last year, I swore I'd never set foot in that classroom again.

But I was in hot pursuit of a crimson kiss, so I grabbed my book bag and said, "Let's go!"

We entered Room 512 to curious looks from Justin and his friends. They were obviously thinking, *What are* they *doing here?* and Travis Ung actually volunteered, "Mr. Webber's not here."

"Good," I laughed, and pulled up a seat next to Justin.

"Wassup?" he asked.

I took his hand and wrote my phone number on his palm.

"It's vanishing ink," I whispered in his ear. "Use it tonight, or it disappears."

Then I grabbed Adrienne and left.

21

Rendezvous

"Wow," Adrienne gasped as we hurried away. "You have become so gutsy!"

I giggled. "Is this living a fantasy or what?"

"No kidding!" She hesitated. "But what if he doesn't call?"

"Then I won't have wasted a bunch of time pining over someone who doesn't have my crimson kiss!"

Fortunately, this was not a problem.

He called at 7:02.

"Hey, Evangeline, it's Justin. Wassup?"

All of a sudden my mouth went dry. But I managed to sound passably confident as I said, "Meet me at the Prager Park gazebo in fifteen minutes."

"Why?"

My mouth now felt stuffed with cotton. "Hmm. If you have to ask, maybe you shouldn't come."

Had that even been intelligible? And what was I *thinking*? What if he said, "Why would I want to meet up with *you*?" How embarrassing would that be?

But then my ear buzzed with the sweet sound of "I'll be there."

I hung up, greatly relieved.

And slightly shocked!

It worked!

I was going to be meeting a romantic guy at a romantic setting.

We were going to do some romantic crimson kissing!

Since Prager Park is only a five-minute walk from the condo, I had plenty of time to take out some crimson-kissing insurance. I refreshed my lip gloss and mascara, then sprayed on some of my mother's musky perfume. It was sultry and very . . . smooth.

It occurred to me as I was spritzing my neck that there was no mention of Delilah's wearing sexy perfumes in *A Crimson Kiss*. It also occurred to me that if she did wear perfume, it would probably be more flowery than musky.

"Who cares?" I said out loud, then stalled for another ten minutes. Showing up five minutes late would be cool. Showing up five minutes early would not.

By the time I left the condo, I was completely giddy. It was a beautiful clear night with a nearly full moon; the air was crisp but not cold, I was meeting a dark-eyed, dashing-looking guy at a gazebo. . . . I actually twirled around twice as I strolled down the sidewalk. I wasn't just seeing a fantasy, I was actually living one!

Unfortunately, when I strolled up to the gazebo, I discovered that Justin Rodriguez had not yet arrived. The setting *was* perfect, but I couldn't enjoy the moonlight, or the sweet smell of honeysuckle, or the cool night air. Instead, I stood around for what seemed like an eternity feeling like a total dweeb and picked at a cuticle. I hate when I rip cuticles. They get all bleedy and oozy and gross. But once I start, I can't seem to stop until the whole thing's torn off.

By the time Justin appeared (out of nowhere, scaring the hell out of me), I'd ripped away the entire cuticle of my left thumb, worrying that I'd been stood up.

"Wassup?" Justin said, acting a little too cool. He laughed. "Why're you so jumpy?"

I almost snapped, "Why are you so late?" but in my head it sounded (*eeew*) desperate. So I leaned against a post of the gazebo and tried for something relaxed and witty. "Jumpy? Maybe I'm a rabbit?"

The second it left my lips, my brain screamed, *A rabbit? What kind of insane thing is that to say? What do you think he's going to read into that? He sure won't think you mean fuzzy and cute!*

He laughed and moved toward me.

"I didn't mean it like that," I said, taking a step away.

"Then why're we here?"

My thumb was oozing and it was distracting me. So I put my thumbnail up to my mouth, trying to look casual as I licked it. The taste of blood mixed with micro specks of Colgate. *Oh, no!* I thought. *It's seriously bleeding!*

Justin's nose started twitching like a rabbit's, and at first I thought he was making fun of me, but then his eyes squeezed together and he let out a loud, splattering sneeze.

A horn beeped from the parking lot behind me as Justin blasted another splattery sneeze into his sleeve. I glanced over my shoulder, then did a double take as two guys dived for cover inside an old Nissan. "You brought Blaine and Travis?"

"Aaaa-chooooo!" He wiped his face. "Your perfume . . . the

flowers . . . something's killin' me!" He twitched and sniffed. *"Aaaa-chooooo!"*

"Why'd you bring Blaine and Travis?"

"Aaaa-chooooo! Why'd you wear that stupid perfume? *Aaaa-chooooo!* Why'd you pick this stupid place? *Aaaa-chooooo!"*

I stared at him. So much for the perfect setting. Obviously there'd be no kissing tonight!

22

Morning Madness

WHEN ADRIENNE AND I WERE EIGHTH GRADERS, we had four out of six classes together. When we moved up to high school, we had only two classes the same, and we thought it was torture. But as sophomores we were down to one class (P.E.), and now we have none. We do have the same teachers for American literature and world history, but they're at different times, so that's only useful for comparing homework answers.

We used to walk to school together, too, but that was before the separation. Now, instead of living a block away from the Willows, I'm at the condo, over a mile away. And this year, while I had my nose in a book (either text or romance) or was killing time at Groove Records, Adrienne was getting more and more involved in school. Newspaper production, which she has first period (and, it seems, at lunch and after school), and choir now ruled her life. If she wasn't rushing off to meet some deadline for the *Larkmont Times,* she was catering to the demanding whims of Mr. and Mrs. Vogel, her choir teachers.

So not seeing her in the quad the morning following the gazebo disaster was nothing unusual.

Her not having called me back the night before was.

Where was she?

I was in the middle of a kissing crisis!

I needed my best friend!

I tried the newspaper production classroom and asked the advisor, Ms. Pickney, if she'd seen her.

"Not this morning, no." As I turned to go, she called, "But when you find her, tell her she should be here! Her page is still half empty! Our deadline is Thursday!"

I waved an acknowledgment, then walked over to the Performance Pavilion, trying to ignore all the couples sucking face in alcoves along the way.

One of the back entrances to the theater was unlocked, and I entered to the sound of angelic voices and a tinkling piano. I found a seat in the shadows and watched as Adrienne and about twenty other singers did vocal gymnastics while Mr. Vogel waved a baton around like he was fending off a swarm of bees and Mrs. Vogel played with exaggerated drama at the baby grand. (They both always dress and act like they're giving the performance of a lifetime. Swooping bows, flowing scarves, polished dress shoes . . . even their hallway "good mornings" are overly theatrical. It's really quite exhausting being around them.)

After a while I found myself watching a tall blond who was standing in the row behind Adrienne. His name was Patrick or Patton or Peyton or . . . some other P name . . . and he was obviously very serious about his singing. Big ooooos, wide eeeees . . . He was hand-some in a choirboy sort of way and had, I decided, a very expressive mouth.

The warning bell rang, and after a brief pep talk from Mr. Vogel about the "fast-approaching spring choral performance," the choir dispersed.

"Adrienne!" I called, hurrying up to the stage.

"Evangeline!" she called back, her cheeks glowing from her early-morning vocalizing. She scampered down the side steps and said, "I'm so sorry I didn't get back to you last night. I fell asleep at eight o'clock, if you can believe that! I was just exhausted." She grabbed my arm and whispered, "So what happened? Did you meet Justin? Did you get your crimson kiss?"

I scowled. "I was so wrong about him. It was a disaster."

"See ya, Adrienne," the blond choirboy said as he went by. "Hey, Evangeline."

"Hey," I said back, racking my brains for his name.

"See ya, Paxton," Adrienne said, her cheeks still glowing.

I did a mental snap of the fingers. *Paxton.*

Adrienne called, "You sounded great today!" after him, then latched on to me again and whispered, "Why was it a disaster? Tell me! Tell me everything!"

"He's allergic to perfume. Or flowers. Or both! He was late, he sneezed all over the place, and get this—he brought Blaine and Travis!"

"No!"

"Seriously. How mature is that? They were spying from his car!"

"Get out!" She gave me a friendly shove, then started making a beeline toward her first-period class. "So . . . no kiss?"

"Not even close." I cut away from her, saying, "I gotta go. Fieldman's the tardy Nazi."

"Are you giving him a second chance?"

I pulled a horrified face. "No!"

She laughed and called, "I'll meet you in the quad at break, okay?" She stopped short. "No, wait! Meet me in Ms. Pickney's room! My page is only half done and the deadline's Thursday! I need every second I can get!"

I called, "Right!" and hurried off with a smile and a wave.

23

Hippity-Hop!

THE BIG SURPRISE DURING MATH was having to avoid eye contact with Robbie Marshall. After the fish kiss he'd totally ignored me, which was more than fine with me. But now suddenly he was watching me, grinning slyly at me, casually flexing his biceps.

What was up with that?

After class I got my question answered.

"You want to go out?" he asked, catching my arm as he whispered it in my ear.

I pulled away. "Uh . . . no."

"Aw, c'mon. We'd be good together."

I stopped and turned to face him. "What about Sunshine?"

He shrugged. "We're kinda broken up."

"*Kinda* broken up?"

"Look," he whispered, "we could just try it out. . . . She doesn't have to know!"

I gave him an Adriennesque squint. "You're disgusting, you know that?" Then I huffed off.

Stu Dillard was the one who provided some clarity to Robbie's sudden renewed interest in me. "Hippity-hop, Evangeline!" he called as I approached Mr. Anderson's world history boredom tomb. Then he put his index fingers up like devil's horns and wiggled them.

At first I didn't get it, but as I slid into my seat, a wave of nausea knocked me flat.

It couldn't be!

I hadn't even *done* anything!

But what else could the wiggly ears and hippity-hop comment be about?

Justin Rodriguez had been talking rabbits!

24

Shack Attack

THERE WAS NO WAY I COULD CONCENTRATE in world history. If Stu knew, so did half the school.

Talk about rabbits—I wanted to crawl into a hole and die!

I couldn't believe it. How could this have happened? Overnight I'd gotten a reputation?

I hadn't even *done* anything!

And there was no way I was going to let some sneezy twerp and his pint-sized posse talk trash about me! At break I stormed around until I found Justin on his way to the Snack Shack.

"What's the big idea?" I asked, and I actually pushed his chest with both my hands.

He stumbled back a step and grinned. "Whoa!"

"Stop that!" I snapped, because I hated the smug way he was looking at me. "I can't believe you told people what I said. You know I didn't mean it that way! You startled me and it just popped out of my mouth!"

He gave a little twitch of the shoulder. "I didn't broadcast it. I just told Blaine and Travis."

"Yeah? Well Stu Dillard called out 'Hippity-hop' to me this morning, so someone somewhere's broadcasting!"

He said, "Sorry," like he couldn't care less. Then he shook his head and said, "I still don't really get why you wanted to meet me—"

I was so exasperated and so *mad* that I just blurted out, "I wanted a kiss. That's all! Just one perfect kiss. And for some insane reason I thought *you* could deliver it! But instead, you delivered your obnoxious little friends and disgusting *sneezes*. And now I have to—"

Before I could finish my rant, he grabbed me, pulled me toward him, and planted a kiss.

Only he kind of missed.

His lips were half on my lips and half off, which was really awkward. And he tried to adjust, but it was just . . . wrong.

Besides, I didn't want him to kiss me on the outskirts of the Snack Shack! I'd wanted him to kiss me in a gazebo in the moonlight. I'd wanted tender, melting lips. A *fantasy* kiss.

This kiss wasn't crimson!

It was a murky, muddled gray!

I tried to pull away from him, but he had his hands clamped on my upper arms and bent forward to stay connected.

I felt a surge of panic.

I was trapped!

Held hostage by a crooked kiss!

When pulling back only made him bend farther forward, I twisted my head to the side and jerked free. But in the process I lost my balance, staggered backward, and fell against an overflowing trash can.

I went down with a *crash*, knocking garbage everywhere.

One look at me sprawled across trash and Justin took off.

That crummy crooked kisser just ditched me!

And the whole Snack Shack line was now staring at me!

I tried to make a graceful return to an upright position, but that wasn't easy with nacho sauce smeared everywhere.

Then someone grabbed my arm to help me up, and I found myself face to face with . . . a Boy Scout?

He wasn't exactly in uniform, but his white polo shirt was tucked into his tan pants, and his whole demeanor was squeaky-clean. His hair was actually *parted* and plastered across his head like he was preparing for a midlife comb-over.

"Thanks," I said, standing up. I was a good six inches taller than he was.

"Are you okay?" he asked.

I nodded and brushed myself off, then watched while he righted the can and scooped the trash back inside. "There," he said when he was done. He looked at his hands and smiled. "I guess I'd better go wash up!"

"Uh, thanks," I said again, giving a lame wave as he hurried off. "Me too."

People in the Snack Shack line were still staring.

I slunk away, thinking that at least now they had something besides rabbits to gossip about.

25

Faulty Analysis

I WAS TARDY TO SPANISH. I'm never tardy to anything, but I was way tardy to Spanish. I'd been looking for Adrienne. It was the only thing I could think to do after escaping the Snack Shack. I looked in Ms. Pickney's room but was told she'd already left for her third-period class. So I hurried over to Room 814, the choir classroom.

The first person I ran into was Paxton.

"Where's Adrienne?" I panted.

"She's running an errand for Mr. Vogel." He cocked his head a bit. "You okay? What happened to your clothes? Is that nacho sauce?"

Clarinets were squeaking in the band room next door. Someone was pounding on a bass drum. "I'm late," I said, and ran to class.

Spanish was a blur. So was American lit. I couldn't stop thinking about Justin's cockeyed kiss. And thrashing in trash. And Robbie Marshall asking me out. And Studly doing devilish bunny ears.

I was living a nightmare, not a fantasy!

What did a girl have to do to get a decent kiss?

Could it possibly be worth *this*?

When the lunch bell rang, I was dying to track down Adrienne, but Miss Ryder held me back. "Evangeline! Can I see you a minute?"

Miss Ryder had told us on the first day of school that she was twenty-three and that it was only her second year teaching. "That's why I'm going to be unfailingly strict—I will take no bull from any of you. I am also unfailingly passionate about literature—it's my life, and I'm looking forward to sharing it with you."

True to her word, she's in love with books. Her cheeks flush when she talks about them, and she goes off on these amazingly eloquent jags about the significance of books. Sometimes, though, I think she sees things *because* she's in love, not because it's really there. Case in point: According to her analysis, *The Last of the Mohicans* is a vehicle for conveying great courage, great treachery, and great love.

According to *my* analysis, it's a story about war.

Anyway, when the rest of the class had stampeded out, she analyzed *me* through her narrow, black-framed, rectangular glasses and said, "You've seemed distracted in class lately. Especially today. Are you doing all right?"

What was I? An open book? "I'm fine," I told her, slamming down the cover.

She held my gaze. "You don't seem fine." There was a moment of awkward silence before she looked away and said, "People talk, Evangeline. It's wrong, but that's what they do."

My jaw hit the floor. My *teacher* had heard?

But . . . exactly *what* had she heard?

"The gossip is really not what's important," she said, looking at me again through those mind-reading lenses. "Just don't do anything *you're* ashamed of—that's my rule of thumb."

"I haven't!" I said, picking my jaw off the floor. "I have done absolutely nothing wrong, or scandalous, or . . . or even remotely nasty!"

Her hands swept upward. "Well, there you go. So just hold your head high, and get on with your life."

I headed for the door.

"But if you ever need someone to talk to . . ."

"Thanks," I said, then scrambled out of there to find Adrienne.

I *had* to find Adrienne.

26

Plenty of Mouth to Go Around

I WENT DIRECTLY TO THE NEWSPAPER PRODUCTION CLASSROOM, but Adrienne wasn't there. I checked the choir room (it was locked); then I full-on *ran* back toward Ms. Pickney's room. I never run through the halls. It's so uncool. But I had to find Adrienne!

In my hurry, I plowed right into Brody, who was emerging from a room in the science wing.

"Have you seen your sister?" I panted as I untangled myself from him.

He shook his head. "Choir? Newspaper? Quad?"

"No, no, and I don't think so . . . but I'll check!" I waved and called, "Thanks, Bro!" and hurried toward the quad.

It didn't make sense that she'd be there, because she had so much else going on, but when I rounded the corner and looked at "our" place, there she was.

"Finally!" she said when I approached. "Where have you been?"

"Looking all over for you!"

"What happened with Justin and the trash can? It can't possibly be as bad as people are making it sound!"

"Oh my God, this *school,*" I cried. I zeroed in on her. "How about rabbits? Are they also talking about rabbits?"

"What? No! What *happened*?"

"I went off on Justin for spreading rumors, and he grabbed me and kissed me. Right by the Snack Shack! But he *missed,* and then he wouldn't let go! So I jerked away from him and wound up falling and knocking over a trash can."

She gasped. "Oh, how embarrassing!" Then she squinted at me and said, "He *missed*? How could he miss? He's got plenty of mouth to go around!"

"You can say *that* again! Him and Travis and Blaine all do!"

"Wait . . . you kissed *them,* too?"

"No! I meant that Travis and Blaine have been mouthing off about last night, too!"

"But . . ." She squinted harder and shook her head. "Where do *rabbits* come in?"

I put a hand to my forehead. "Last night Justin was late, he startled me, and when he asked why I was so jumpy, out of my brilliant mouth came 'Maybe I'm a rabbit?' "

Adrienne laughed, then put both hands in front of her face and peeked at me over the tops of her fingertips. "No!"

"Yes! And somehow Stu found out and he's been 'hippity-hopping' when he sees me! Which is why I went off on Justin!"

She shook her head, then grabbed me by the arm and said, "I've got a deadline, and you're coming with me. I don't think it's safe to leave you alone anymore."

So I let her lead me toward Ms. Pickney's room. I already felt a lot better, but mostly I felt grateful that Adrienne Willow was my friend.

27

Surrealistic Pillow

After school I holed up at Groove Records. For me, walking through that door is like opening *A Crimson Kiss*. I enter and escape.

Usually I just meander around the store. I read the backs of ancient LPs, listen to some obscure band Izzy's got pumping into every nook of the store, or relax on a thrasher couch reading tattered back issues of *Rolling Stone*.

And usually there are at least a couple other people in the store doing the same thing I am, or trying out used guitars in the guitar room, but this time the place seemed deserted. There wasn't even any music playing.

Izzy was near the register, changing the strings of his guitar. "Hey, Bubbles!" he called.

"Hey, Izzy," I called back, then cupped my hand behind my ear and scanned the air. "I can't believe what I'm not hearing!"

He laughed and put down his string-winding tool. "Guess I was preoccupied, sorry! I'll get some music spinnin'."

So I was walking down the corridor between crates of LPs when suddenly it was like someone pushed me from behind.

It *wasn't* a push.

It wasn't even a person.

It was a *voice*.

When the truth is found to be lies . . . and all the joy . . . within you . . . dies . . . don't you want somebody to love? Don't you need somebody to love? Wouldn't you love somebody to love? You better find somebody to love . . . love.

I moved toward a speaker that was mounted near the ceiling, mesmerized. It was the clearest, strongest female voice I'd ever heard. And as the song went on, I just stood there gaping up at that . . . *voice.*

It was a short song, over way before I wanted it to be. So I hurried up to the counter and asked Izzy, "Who *was* that?"

He looked up from his guitar surgery. "Grace Slick. Jefferson Airplane."

The next song had started, but it wasn't anything like the other one. "Can you play that first song again?"

"Sure," he said, pushing back his glasses. "Your old man never played Jefferson Airplane for you?"

I shook my head.

"I can't believe that." He picked up the needle and carefully placed it back on the LP. "They wimped out when they became Jefferson Starship, but this is untouchable sixties gold."

There was a moment of silence and then that *voice*. No introduction, no warning, just that *voice*.

"Wow," I said when it was over. "Is it called 'Somebody to Love'?"

Izzy nodded as he pulled the needle up again. "You'll like this one, too," he said, then grinned at me. " 'White Rabbit.' "

" 'White *Rabbit*'? No! Don't play anything about rabbits!"

He gave me a funny look. "You've got something against rabbits?"

"Uh . . . can you just play 'Somebody to Love' again?"

So he did, and when it was over, I asked, "Do you have that on CD?"

"I think I might," he said, and led me over to the used CD section.

It took a while, but eventually he handed over a jewel box. *"Surrealistic Pillow?"* I asked, blinking at the five guys and one girl on the cover.

He nodded and grinned. "Gotta love the sixties."

I followed him back to the register. I didn't care when it was made. I just wanted, no, I *needed* that song.

28

Reflections

THE NEXT DAY AT SCHOOL I started lying low, meeting up with Adrienne wherever her commitments required her to be. It felt safe, but after a day and a half I began hating it. Adrienne was so busy, so *involved*. Obsessing over 'Somebody to Love' and *A Crimson Kiss* did not qualify as having a life!

And even though the three kisses I'd gotten hadn't been anywhere near crimson, at least I'd *felt* something in their pursuit. I'd looked forward to school. I'd looked forward to sparks flying. I'd looked forward to the *possibility*.

Following Adrienne around everywhere made me feel like I was backsliding. This was her life I was living, not mine. It was a different jacket on the same sad story!

So at lunch while she was typing like mad at the computer to finish a newspaper article, I collected my things and snuck out without her even noticing.

I meandered away from the classrooms toward the quiet outskirts of campus, and when I found a little patch of grass in a remote corner near the 300 wing, I sat down, took a deep breath, then opened my book bag and pulled out *A Crimson Kiss*.

I read through some of my favorite passages, but it didn't take long for me to see that Grace Slick was right—I did need somebody to love!

But . . . how was I going to "find somebody to love"?

Reading a romance novel on the outskirts of campus was sure not doing the trick! And after giving it some thought, I realized that the cure was actually obvious:

I needed to pull myself up by the bootstraps.

I needed to get back on that horse!

I needed to try again.

After all, this was a big school. How could I have given up so easily?

It was time to lube my lips and get back out there!

Crimson kissing might be right around the corner.

29

Chemistry Lesson

I WAS TARDY TO CHEMISTRY. I guess the bells don't ring very loudly in remote corners of the 300 wing.

Who knew?

But I didn't care. I was preoccupied with my renewed quest and my lunchtime reading. Like a backdrop to my thoughts, one particular passage from *A Crimson Kiss* looped through my mind:

> *"Delilah." Now that he had found her, the words he'd so painstakingly planned eluded him. And then, like a knife through his heart, Grayson saw that she had been crying. "Delilah . . . ," he whispered again, this time reaching out to trace the path of a remnant tear.*

Where were the Graysons of Larkmont High?

Where were the tender lips and fervid hearts?

They had to be somewhere!

"Evangeline," Mr. Kiraly said in his heavy Hungarian accent, "you're tardy." He put a black mark in his grade book. "That's one of three allotted tardies for the semester."

I nodded an acknowledgment.

After he'd finished documenting my infraction, he lifted his dandruff-heavy buzz cut and leveled a gaze at the class. "Clear your desks, people."

I froze. We were having a quiz?

I looked around, but nobody else seemed shocked.

"Number your answer sheets from one to thirty. Number your work as well. I will give partial credit, but not if I cannot find your work!"

My jaw dropped as test packets floated toward me along the row. This was no pop quiz, this was a full-on test! How had I missed knowing about this?

Chemistry is one of my best subjects. Electrons and protons and covalent bonding make total sense to me. I've got Avogadro's number and molar conversions and net ionic equations *down.*

But that's because I've studied. That's because I've *tried.* That's because all year I've actually read the chapters and done the section reviews to prepare for tests. Nobody else I know bothers with the section reviews! Why do them if they're not assigned?

But I'd barely skimmed this chapter. I hadn't done any section reviews. I didn't even know we'd completed the chapter!

How could this be?

I took my test packet and passed the rest of them to Roper Harding behind me. "When did he announce a test?" I whispered.

Roper gave me a strange look. "Shhh!" he said in a real worried way, and pointed to the front board.

A banner of yellow chalk stating CHAPTER TEST THURSDAY was clearly visible across the top of the board.

"When did he put that up there?" I whispered to Roper, because I was still gripped by denial.

"Shhh!" he answered.

I took in his oversized glasses, oily hair, and acne, and snorted.

He wouldn't know a remnant tear if it splashed him in the zit!

Then I turned around and bombed the test.

30

The Psychology of It All

I SPENT THE LAST PERIOD OF THE DAY stunned over what had happened in chemistry. Concentrating on Mr. Stills's lecture in psychology might have been wiser, but I felt I understood the concepts of "sour grapes" and "displaced aggression" well enough, so I tuned him out and obsessed about chemistry.

That is, until Andrew Prescott caught my eye.

"You okay?" he mouthed.

First Paxton and now him? Since when do guys ask if someone's okay? Guys are usually the *cause* of girls not feeling okay, which is why it's counter-anthropological and wholly unnatural for them to ask the question.

Then Andrew Prescott slipped me a note.

Hello?

A *note*?

Curiosity got the better of me. I unfolded it and read *You seem totally bummed.*

I raised an eyebrow in his direction, then scribbled, *I bombed a chemistry test,* and passed the note back.

He smirked and wrote, *Who didn't? It was tough.*

You have Kiraly? I wrote back. *What period?*

He started to scribble a reply, but suddenly Mr. Stills was looming above him with his hand out.

Without a word, Mr. Stills read the note, pocketed it, then continued his lecture. Andrew and I exchanged looks, and by the end of class I'd convinced myself that that was the end of it—there'd be no repercussions.

Then the dismissal bell rang.

"Mr. Prescott, Miss Logan . . . up here, please," Mr. Stills commanded.

We shuffled over to the podium, where he looked directly at me and said, "I take it from your lack of focus today that chemistry is a more important subject to you than psychology?"

From his tone, Mr. Stills obviously had some issues regarding psychology's place in the hierarchy of sciences. And the truth is I did think his course was mostly filler, but psych is one of my few easy A's, and I didn't want him to start sabotaging my grade (subconsciously or otherwise) because he resented the hard sciences. And since I don't like to lie, I avoided his question altogether. "I'm sorry, Mr. Stills. I was just really bummed about my chemistry test last period. Andrew noticed and tried to make me feel better. You understand that, right? It doesn't have anything to do with your class."

He chewed on that a minute, then nodded and said, "School's out—go home. Just don't let it become a habit." But as we were leaving, he chucked the note in the trash and said, "Someday you'll see that all the physics and chemistry and calculus in the world won't serve you as well as an understanding of behavioral psychology."

"Thanks," I said, not feeling at all grateful.

"Sorry I got you in trouble," Andrew said once we were outside.

"Don't sweat it," I said, turning to face him.

And that's when it struck me—Andrew Prescott has lips!

Truly *outstanding* lips.

Even, full, moist . . . classic, movie-star lips.

And through my mind swept the realization that he'd been sensitive.

And kind.

And those *lips* . . .

How could I have never noticed those lips?

Suddenly I couldn't resist the magnetic pull of his magnificent mouth.

It tugged me in closer.

And closer.

Until I just gave in and kissed him.

31

Driven

THE PROBLEM WITH KISSING ANDREW PRESCOTT wasn't that I shocked him. Or that it was obvious after about two seconds that his perfect movie-star lips had probably never kissed a girl before. Or even that once we'd started, he didn't want to stop.

No, the real problem was that Stu Dillard saw us kissing.

"Hippity-*hop*," he whooped from across the way.

I broke free from Andrew and shouted, "Get a life, Stu!" then took off in the opposite direction.

Andrew chased after me. "Evangeline, wait! Where're you going?"

"Sorry," I said, marching along. "I probably shouldn't have done that. I was just trying to say thanks for . . . I don't know . . . caring, I guess."

"But . . ." He marched along beside me. "At least let me say you're welcome?"

I stopped and looked at him, because how cute was that? But I shook my head and said, "I'm sorry. I didn't mean it the way you took it. It was a one-kiss deal."

"But . . ."

"I've got to go, Andrew. I'll see you tomorrow."

I knew Adrienne was staying after school to work on a newspaper deadline, but instead of going over to Ms. Pickney's classroom to tell her what had happened, I just headed for home. I was feeling a little strange about having kissed Andrew, and I was still totally bummed about my chemistry test.

So I started toward the condo. But after I'd walked about three blocks, a familiar purring motor eased up to the curb beside me.

Brody rolled down the passenger-side window and called, "You want a ride?"

I got in. "Just don't ask me how I am, all right? I might puke."

"Wouldn't want that," he said with a little smile. Then did a textbook Signal-Mirror-Over-Go maneuver back into traffic.

"You are so law-abiding," I grumbled, turning on the radio.

He blushed. "And you're not?"

"No." I slouched. "Well, yeah, I suppose I am." I squirmed. "No, I take that back—I'm not." I squirmed the other way. "Hell, I don't know."

He chuckled. "Well, put your seat belt on. I don't want a ticket." He glanced at me. "Or for you to get hurt."

I snorted as I buckled up. "Planning to crash into something?"

He shrugged. "No, but that doesn't mean I won't."

I closed my eyes and leaned my head against the seat, letting the backbeat of the White Stripes massage my nerves. "Just drive, Chevy-man. Just drive."

32

Cool Compression

FRIDAY MORNING I WOKE UP LATE and had annoyingly puffy eyes. I hate waking up with puffy eyes. Just seeing myself with pink clouds of skin around my eyes wipes me out.

Not that I wasn't wiped out already. I just hadn't been able to sleep. Crummy and confusing kissing aside, I was really upset about chemistry. I'd worked so hard to have a solid A in that class, and now my grade was, without a doubt, in the B zone. And since Mr. Kiraly doesn't give extra credit, it would be a major struggle to earn back my A.

All those nights studying, all that extra effort, for what?

A lousy B.

Anyway, for puffy eyes, I'm a fan of the herbal cold compress. We keep one at the ready in the fridge, so I sat at the kitchen table and strapped it on, then blindly spooned Frosted Mini-Wheats into my mouth.

This was an easily managed form of before-school multitasking until the phone rang. I jumped, shooting milk and cereal everywhere.

I cursed, whipped off the compress, located the phone, and jabbed the talk button so the ringing wouldn't wake up my mother. "What's up?" I whispered, thinking it was Adrienne. After all, who else would call at such an ungodly hour?

"Evangeline?" my dad's voice said in a hesitant, surprised-to-find-you-at-home fashion. "Shouldn't you be on your way to school?"

"Shouldn't you be minding your own business?" I replied.

"Look. I just wanted to leave a message. Could you tell your mother that something's come up and I can't meet her for breakfast? And that I'm very sorry?"

I hesitated. "Wait. Let me get this straight. You called her up to wake her up to *stand* her up?"

"I'm not standing her up! That's why I'm calling."

"Whatever." I clicked off the phone, plopped into my chair, and slapped the compress back on my face.

Stupid, puffy eyes.

33

More Notes

I WAS ACTUALLY *NOT* LATE TO FIRST PERIOD. Mrs. Fieldman's classroom is on the outskirts of campus nearest the condo, and the school's side gate was open due to the reconstruction they're doing to our crumbling campus. (Bulldozers are the real answer, but nobody's asking me.)

So I was feeling lucky to have slid into my seat moments before the final bell, but that didn't last long. A note was delivered shortly after class started, and after inspecting it, Mrs. Fieldman said, "Evangeline, for you," and motioned me to her desk.

It was a small, official-looking blue note, folded neatly in half.

An image of the not-so-official-looking scrap of paper I'd taped to the toilet lid with *The jerk can't meet you for breakfast* scrawled on it flashed through my mind as I returned to my seat.

I sat at my desk, holding the note, staring at the adult script of my name, black ink against blue paper. I finally opened it and discovered that it was just Mr. Hikks, my counselor. He wanted to see me at break.

But . . . why? He'd never summoned me before. *I* was the one who made appointments with *him,* not the other way around. He was much too busy dealing with flunkies to worry about which colleges I should apply to, or what scholarships I might be eligible for.

"Pass your homework to the right," Mrs. Fieldman commanded. "Points off on *your* homework for any missed corrections. There's been a rash of that lately."

Unfortunately, Sandra Herrera was absent again. "Hey, Robbie," I said, sighing.

"What's the deal with you?" he whispered hoarsely. "Me, Rodriguez, and *Prescott,* bam-bam-bam?"

My first thought was *How did he hear about Andrew?* My second thought was *I hate this school!* And my third thought was *What do you mean, bam-bam-bam?* It had been over a week since his mouth had mangled mine!

I wanted to correct him, but I turned to his paper and corrected that instead. And as Mrs. Fieldman called out the answers, I noticed that the majority of Robbie's were right, but that his work didn't support his answers. It annoyed me, but really, why should I care? Everyone knew how the game was played: He'd get into college on an athletic scholarship, he'd major in jockology, and if he played well, he'd graduate and come back to high school to teach P.E., passing on the pressure to let jocks slide. One dummied homework paper was nothing in the scheme of things.

But the farther down the paper I graded, the more disgusted I felt. Why, oh, *why* had I ever wanted this moron to kiss me?

After class I hurried through the door, but Robbie grabbed me by the arm and pulled me aside. "I seriously want to know what your deal is. Why'd you come on to me that day?"

I twisted free of him. "What's *your* deal? Just drop it, would you?"

I escaped to second period, relieved for once to be spending time in the world history boredom tomb.

34

Counseling

"TELL ME," DELILAH WHISPERED. "Tell me where I can go to escape these memories, these ghosts."

"I'll show you," he told her. And then, with a tenderness that belied his imposing physique, Grayson took her hand.

Grayson didn't take Delilah to the counselor's office. (Or to bed, like in most of those ridiculous books my mom has.) He took her to a park bench overlooking a serene lake that had swans gliding along it and "graceful weeping willow boughs aching to taste the glistening water."

I shifted in my oh-so-comfy formed plastic chair as I waited outside Mr. Hikks's closed office door thinking that some lovely swans and glistening water would do wonders for my mood. Actually, at this point some basic air-conditioning would help. Why was it so hot in here? It was beautiful outside . . . why couldn't we open some windows?

"Are you sure he's in there?" I asked the counselors' secretary. I knew he was, but I was tired of wasting my break in this stifling place.

She nodded. "It'll only be another minute, I'm sure. And I know it's important, Evangeline, so just sit tight."

I went to the Sparkletts dispenser and treated myself to a paper cup of room-temperature water. How did she know it was important? Who had been talking to whom? Was this about the few recent blips on my otherwise shining academic record? Had my teachers alerted Mr. Hikks to my lack of focus? My newfound test-bombing abilities?

Or . . .

Was this about . . .

Kissing?

My blood pressure went up fast. My head started swimming with the sudden realization that my summons to the counselor's office might be for actual *counseling*.

But . . . did they really think I'd talk to Mr. Hikks?

That I'd be able to explain anything during a twenty-minute nutrition break?

Who were these people, and what had they done with reality?

Mr. Hikks's door opened. A purple-mohawked Ryce Tibbins strode out sporting ripped black cotton, multiple piercings, and military boots.

We exchanged nods, and at the last minute he tagged on a knowing sneer.

Why the sneer? I asked myself as he bashed through the reception-area door. Had he seen my graceful dive into garbage the other day?

Had he heard about my . . .

Kissing?

"Evangeline?" Mr. Hikks said with an artificial smile. "Come in."

So into his cubby of clutter I went.

"How are you?"

"Fine," I said, standing in front of his desk. There were stacks of papers, transcripts, college catalogs, newspapers, file folders . . . the place was a disaster.

He swigged back some coffee and grimaced like it was bitter or cold, or maybe both. "Have a seat."

"What's this about?" I asked, not sitting. "I really don't want to be late to Spanish."

He flipped open a manila folder with my name on it. "I'll write you a note. Have a seat."

My knees wimped out on me.

I sat.

"We've sent three letters home about this," he began, then took another swig of the sludge in his coffee mug.

My mind raced. Three letters home? *Already?* Why hadn't I seen them? And what about the flunkies? What about all the seniors in danger of not graduating? What about the bathroom smokers, for that matter! The drug dealers! The people who scrawl obscene messages inside bathroom stalls? What about them? So I'd kissed a couple of guys. So I'd bombed a test. So I'd been a little distracted.

So *what*?

Mr. Hikks thumped his coffee mug on his desk, looked me directly in the eye, and said, "You need to do your community-service hours, Evangeline. We will not advance you to senior status if you haven't completed your community-service hours." He frowned at me. "Even if you do have nearly a four point oh." He shoved a paper in front of me. "Here's a copy of the list we've mailed to you *three times*."

I picked up the paper and looked it over. I could feel myself flush with a strange, almost uncontrollable anger. I'd been totally stressing out in the waiting area for *this*?

"Just choose an organization and get your hours done," he snapped.

I leveled a look at him. "Mr. Hikks, I never got this paper in the mail."

"Well, now you have it, don't you?"

His sarcastic tone ticked me off even more. Why was he treating me like a delinquent? Didn't my hard-earned GPA entitle me to a little respect? Couldn't he at least be a little more . . . pleasant?

My whole body felt flushed, but I tried to stay calm. "Mr. Hikks, my point is, where did you mail it?"

He swiveled in his chair and rattled away at his keyboard, then pointed to an entry on his computer monitor. "Seven sixty-eight Sycamore Drive."

"Well," I said, trembling now with anger, "I don't happen to live there anymore."

He rolled his eyes. *"Well,"* he said back, "it would help if you would inform the school of these things!"

My head felt strangely light. My whole *body* felt like it might just float away. "It would help *more*," I said as I shoved out of my chair, "if you would go to hell!"

Then I stormed out of his office and burst into tears.

35

The Tune of a Hickory Stick

Being out in the fresh air helped me get a grip.

Mr. Hikks was certainly not worth runny mascara!

I took a deep breath, wiped away the tears, and ran to Spanish.

The running was a waste, as I was tardy anyway. And then midway through class a pink note arrived, instructing me to report to Ms. Hershey's office at once.

Ms. Hershey is not sweet, as her name might imply. She has a reputation for being severe and decisive, traits I always thought were necessary (if not commendable) in a vice principal. Miss Ryder calls her the hickory stick of Larkmont High, which, coming from an English teacher, would seem like an innocent enough metaphor, except she always does it with an evil glint in her eye.

So I was definitely not looking forward to meeting Ms. Hershey. How had this happened? How could I, Evangeline Nearly-4.0 Logan, be facing off with the Hickory Stick?

"Sit," Ms. Hershey commanded after I'd been let into her office.

I sat.

"We do not tell our counselors to go to hell," she said, her lips firm, her nostrils slightly flared.

I simply nodded and said, "I know. I'm sorry."

This seemed to throw her.

"Then . . . why did you do it?"

I held her gaze. "I . . . it doesn't matter. I just shouldn't have said it. I'm sorry."

Ms. Hershey continued to stare at me a moment, then turned to her computer and pulled up my stats. "You're an exemplary student," she said, turning back to me. "Your citizenship and work-habit markings are also outstanding. Is there something going on with you?"

"Pardon?"

"Is there some reason you flew off the handle today?"

I looked at my hands for a moment. How could I talk to someone I didn't know about something I couldn't really explain? I shook my head and looked back at her. "It was just wrong, okay? What do I need to do to atone?"

An unexpected smile seemed to tickle her face. "To atone?" She thought for a moment, then breathed in deeply and said, "Considering your track record, I think a note of apology will suffice." She passed me a sheet of paper and a pen, adding, "As long as I have your assurance that it won't happen again."

I nodded.

"So give me your new contact information, write that note, and let's get this unfortunate incident behind us."

So I told her the condo's address and phone number, and on the spot I wrote a conciliatory note to Mr. Hikks.

Inside, though, I felt odd and shaky.

Inside, I wasn't at all sure it wouldn't happen again.

36

News Flash

"PAXTON SAID HE SAW YOU with a pink slip!" Adrienne said as she joined me in the quad at lunch. "I told him he was delusional." She hesitated. "He was delusional, right?"

I dug the summons out of my jeans and handed it over.

"To Ms. Hershey's?" she gasped. "Why?"

I peeled back the wrapper of my lovely Snack Shack burrito. "Because I told Mr. Hikks to go to hell."

"No!" she gasped. "Why?"

"He wasted my whole break over community-service hours. He was so condescending, and it was so hot in there. I felt trapped and . . . I don't know . . . I just lost it."

"Wow . . ."

There was nothing remotely squintlike about Adrienne's expression. Instead, her face seemed to be stretched out in all directions, which was strange. "Look. It's all settled," I said, picking at the disgusting crust of my burrito. "I wrote Mr. Hikks a note and said I was sorry. . . . It's over." I tried a bite of the burrito, chewing on cold beans as I asked, "Do you have any plans for community-service hours?"

"Oh, the Elf Extravaganza took care of that."

"It did?" *I* squinted at *her*. "How is dressing up like elves and singing Christmas songs serving the community?"

"We did performances for the children's hospital, remember?" She heaved a sigh. "Those poor kids. I'd sing for them every day if I could." Then she looked at me and said, "Community hours are easy, Evangeline. Just pick an organization and do it."

"You sound like Mr. Hikks," I grumbled.

She shrugged. "You could also tutor right here at school. That's what Paxton's doing."

"Where?"

"I'll ask him. It's on Tuesdays or Wednesdays, or maybe both. I'll get details." She gave me a mischievous look. "Or you could just ask Mr. Hikks."

"Oh, *right*," I laughed.

"Hey," she asked, suddenly bubbling with excitement, "how'd you like the newspaper?"

"Great issue," I said, although I'd barely had a chance to leaf through it.

Adrienne pulled out her copy of the *Larkmont Times* and held it open, nodding at page three. "You have no idea how hard it was to balance the text and the graphics here. I had this text overflow problem that was just driving me bonkers! And this picture here of Lloyd Morro? It kept disappearing! I'd paste it in, move it to front, *save* it, but poof! The next time I'd open the file, it would be gone."

She nodded at page two. "We got so many paid personals this time! Did you read them? We made a mint on them. I think it's because the Spring Fling is tonight and people are after a last-minute date. Or maybe people just know each other better now. Do you remember how we had, like, *two* at the beginning of the year, and how we had to make some up, just to keep it from being so embarrassing?" She looked at me, her face glowing. "Hey! You should put an ad in— 'Wanted: A crimson kiss.'"

I snorted. "Maybe I should. I sure don't seem to be able to find one on my own."

"Any new prospects?"

I shook my head, and I was about to spill what had happened with Andrew, but before I could find the words, she said, "Do you want to meet me at the dance tonight?"

"You're going to the dance?"

"I've got to cover it for newspaper. Ms. Pickney insists that it's 'important.'"

I gave her one of her own trademark squints. "The Spring Fling is just like every other dance here: It's so loud you can't talk, they play awful music, and it's sweltering in the gym."

"I know. I remember." She shrugged. "But I'm assigned, and that's where I'll be."

"But . . . why you? Isn't someone from newspaper going to the dance, anyway? Why couldn't they just cover it?"

She frowned. "Apparently I'm the only one available." She folded up the *Times* and rifled through her backpack for her sack lunch and bottle of water, grumbling, "That class is full of loafers."

"Well, sorry, but I don't want to tag along."

"I don't blame you." She unwrapped her usual multilayered

sandwich, which was half smashed but still delicious-looking. "So what are you going to do?"

I'd made it to the center of my burrito, which was slightly frozen. "I don't know. This has been one lousy day. I'm just looking forward to it being *over*."

Then I tossed the rest of my burrito in the trash.

37

Counteracting the Mope Gene

MOPING IS COUNTERPRODUCTIVE. Once you start, it'll hook you and drag you down until you are full-on depressed. To counteract my mope gene (which clearly comes from my maternal side), I eat ice cream. I read. I hang out at Groove Records. I shop. I blast music. I go to Adrienne's.

Adrienne was not available, and since there was a note from my mother asking me to wash the dishes and mop the kitchen floor, I settled on the driving, bluesy rock of The Black Crowes and got busy, singing along with "Twice as Hard," "Jealous Again," and "Sister Luck" as I did the dishes. I dried and put away during "Could I've Been So Blind," "Hard to Handle," and "Thick 'n' Thin," mopped the floor through "She Talks to Angels," "Struttin' Blues," and "Stare It Cold," then collected the trash and tidied up until the Crowes were done cawing.

Chores are no big deal when you're rockin' out.

I was actually starting to feel good!

By the time the Spring Fling was scheduled to begin, I'd eaten dinner (a bowl of Cheerios and a big dish of rocky road ice cream), had read from where I'd left off in *A Crimson Kiss*, and was disciplining myself to tackle the section reviews of the material covered in the chemistry test I'd bombed. After I was done with that, I planned to move on to the next section. I wasn't just going to catch up, I was going to get ahead! This was not, N-O-T, going to happen to me again. I was going to be on top of things! Focused!

Unfortunately, galvanic cells and standard electrode potential have got nothing on the meandering thoughts of a girl genetically predisposed to moping. My mind started wandering, thinking about Adrienne at the dance.

About Adrienne having a *life*.

Here I was at home on a Friday night, doing chores and studying chemistry?

Whose fantasy was that?

Not mine!

The phone rang, so I abandoned my chemistry book and dashed into the kitchen to answer it.

"Hi, sweetie!" my mom sang out. "Happy Friday. Just checking in to see what you and Adrienne are up to tonight."

Her calling was a little odd, but it was nice to hear her sounding cheerful. "Adrienne's covering a school function for newspaper, and I'm catching up on my chemistry."

"Chemistry?" There was a pause, then, "So you're not ... getting together?"

This was also a little odd. And I suddenly sensed that there was more to this than a maternal concern over my being nearly seventeen years old, studying chemistry alone on a Friday night.

And then I got it.

"Let me guess. He stood you up for breakfast, so now you're going to have dinner with him after your shift."

There was another pause, then very decisively she said, "He didn't stand me up, Evangeline. And it's for dessert. Dessert and coffee. That's all."

"Mm-hmm."

"But if you're home alone, I'll just cancel. You and I could go out for a bite, or catch a late movie?"

"Forget it, Mom. I'm fine."

"Are you sure?"

"Yup."

But after we said goodbye, I spent the next ten minutes staring at the wall. I wasn't going to be able to concentrate on galvanic cells and standard electrode potential. That was insane!

I needed to get out.

I needed to *do* something.

I needed a life!

Groove Records was closed, and the only place I could think to go was the dance.

38

Memories

As I was getting dressed to go to the dance, I suddenly realized that my first kiss had happened at a school dance. The Beaumont Middle School parents—including my mom—were very "involved," putting on a dance every month, usually on a Friday right after school. So it was convenient to attend dances, but Adrienne and I never went. The truth is, we were afraid.

Were we afraid because we'd never danced outside of P.E. class? (Do-si-do-ing does not really count as dancing.)

Were we afraid we'd be asked to dance by a boy we thought was a total dweeb?

Were we afraid of *being* the total dweebs?

Whatever it was, it wasn't until the eighth-grade promotional dance that our mothers joined forces and said, "You're going. It's not just a dance, it's a party. There'll be plenty of other things to do if you don't want to dance."

We, of course, were dying to dance; we just had never danced with a boy and were afraid that we didn't really know how. So we agonized over what to wear, how to act, and what to say (especially if dweeby boys asked us to dance). And then the Thursday night before the big event, we finally got serious about the actual dancing. We spent hours in my bedroom with the radio on, trying to figure it out.

Mom and Dad thought we were hysterical and tried to demonstrate how to dance fast and then slow. "Although you probably won't be doing any slow dancing," my dad said after they'd taken a few swaying turns around the middle of my room. "Take my word for it—eighth-grade boys are terrified of slow dancing."

This parental coaching may have been well intentioned, but it was more embarrassing than instructive. "My dad doesn't dance," Adrienne whispered into my very receptive ear.

I gave her a nod and said to my still-swaying parents, "Thanks, guys. We get it. We're going to Adrienne's for a while to figure out what to wear."

On the walk over to her house, Adrienne had asked me the one thing I'd been trying to *not* think about: "What if Lucas asks you to dance?"

I shot back with, "What if Noah asks you?"

We both laughed and agreed: "They won't!"

But we were wrong. At least, we were half wrong. Noah was there, but he spent the whole time playing foosball and table tennis in an area they'd cordoned off for alternate activities.

Lucas spent the last three songs dancing with me.

And during the very last seconds of the very last dance, he suddenly moved in and kissed me.

It was sweaty and zip-lipped, but that kiss had me jumping up and down for the entire final week of school. Right up to the time I found out that Lucas's family was moving to Georgia.

"Georgia!" I cried. "What's in *Georgia*?"

"My dad got a promotion," he said, kicking a rock.

I gave him my e-mail, my address, my phone number.

I never heard from him again.

39

The Spit Bath

GRAYSON SWEPT HER GENTLY around the dance floor, his steps confident and light. Soon he was spellbound—her scent, her glow, her delicate touch and crystal-clear eyes—who was this bewitching creature? How had he not noticed her before?

When the music stopped, he held her gaze and, no longer able to resist the impulse, lifted her satin-smooth hand to his lips.

Bolstered by the romantic passage from *A Crimson Kiss*, I reached the school convinced that something wonderful might actually happen. Maybe someone would sweep me off *my* feet. Maybe even deliver a crimson kiss!

I knew it would be hot in the gym, so I'd dressed accordingly, borrowing a red keyhole halter from the depths of one of my mom's clothes boxes. I paid my five bucks at the door, then went inside.

The dance had been under way for over an hour and a half, and the gym was stuffy and dark, lit only by glow sticks and bracelets bobbing to an overdriven beat. I wandered through the crowd looking for Adrienne, and my eyes were still adjusting to the dark when I accidentally thumped into someone.

"Excuse me!" I said.

"Bitch!" was the immediate reply.

Perfect. Hundreds of people in the gym and I manage to hip-check Sunshine Holden.

Sunshine Holden, who, I now noticed, was holding a hand that was attached to an arm that did *not* connect to Robbie Marshall.

No, it belonged to Stu Dillard.

Apparently my jaw had fallen out of its socket, because Sunshine snarled, "Get over it."

"Consider it done," I answered.

"Consider it your fault!" she seethed in my ear as I went by.

"Consider yourself lucky!" I called, then snipped, "Stu's *gotta* be a better kisser!"

I escaped the two of them, threading my way through the crowd, searching for Adrienne. Or any friendly face. Being alone in a crowded gym where everyone else seems to have someone else is so . . . embarrassing. It feels like everyone's staring at you thinking, Don't you have any friends? Couldn't you get a date? Doesn't anyone want to dance with you?

I took a deep breath.

I told myself, Say your fantasy, see your fantasy, *live your fantasy.*

You'll never get a crimson kiss by moping around! This gym is full of guys! Find one! Dance! Have some fun!

There was a warm touch to my elbow. "Evangeline?"

I turned and saw a smiling . . . Blake Jennings? We'd had a few classes together as freshmen, but I couldn't remember having seen him since. He was definitely older, and much hipper-looking.

"Blake?"

"Wow, you look great!" he said, eyeing me up and down.

"Didn't know you still went to school here," I called back over the music.

"I don't! I do still have friends here, though. They invited me. How have you been?"

"Great! You?"

"Great!"

We smiled at each other, sincerely at first, then awkwardly. We'd already run out of things to say.

He looked out at the bobbing glow sticks. "You want to dance?"

He was standing very close to me; his breath was warm and sweet. "Sure," I called back.

The odd thing about dancing is that you're immediately thrown up against someone you may barely know, and it means nothing. Girls wrap themselves around guys, guys latch on to girls, people gyrate like animals, and when the music stops, they separate and walk off like it was no big deal. Do that on campus in the middle of the day and the whole school will be talking, but on the dance floor? No one seems to care.

Anyway, the instant I said "Sure," Blake grabbed my hand and led me into the sea of sweat and overtaxed deodorant. And even though a bass-heavy tune that was not exactly meant for slow dancing was playing, Blake latched on to me and started to sway.

But after a few turns he began nibble-kissing my shoulder, working his way up my neck to my earlobe. Then he started licking the edges of my ear and *huffing* into it.

I pulled away from him, but before long he'd pulled me back, zeroing in on my ear again, this time thrusting his tongue inside it and doing licky laps around it.

Saliva began dripping down my neck.

He was giving me a full-on spit bath!

I was going to get swimmer's ear!

I felt like shouting, "It's an ear, dude! An *ear*," but instead I just broke away.

"What'sa matter?" he asked.

I casually wiped my neck and ear dry and made an attempt at diplomacy: "That was a little intense, is all."

He grinned, totally misinterpreting my comment. "You want to go outside? It's cooler."

I shook my head. "I've . . . I've actually got to find my friend." Then I did what all girls do when they're desperate to escape a guy at a school dance—I made a beeline for the locker room.

40

Interception

ON MY ESCAPE TO THE LOCKER ROOM, I got waylaid by Jasmine Hernandez. Jasmine Hernandez, who hadn't said boo to me since seventh grade. (And whom I haven't wanted to say boo to since she fell in with the fast crowd last year.)

"Are you here with Robbie?" she asked.

"No!" I said, giving her a curl of the lip.

"So you guys aren't going out?"

"No!"

"But I heard he dumped Sunshine because of you! And I saw Sunshine here with Stu!"

I shook my head. "He didn't dump her for me. I want nothing to do with him."

Her jaw dropped. "How can you want nothing to do with him? He is smokin' *hot*."

I shrugged. "Go for it, Jasmine."

I resumed my trek to the locker room, and as I approached, a beacon of locker-room light shone on a girl gliding toward me. What a relief! "Adrienne!"

"I can't believe you're here!" she cried.

"I can't believe it either!"

"Wow, look at you!" she said. "Obviously you're not on a journalism assignment."

I shrugged. "It's a dance."

"So . . . have you danced?" She leaned in. "Have you kissed?"

I pulled her farther away from the locker-room light and told her all about Blake Jennings.

"Eeew," she said. "Ew-ew-ew!"

I shook out my ear. "I need a sponge mop!"

Adrienne laughed. "Spit spill in canal two!"

I laughed, too, then said, "You know, I don't think I'm going to find a crimson kisser here. How long do you have to stay? Can you come over, maybe spend the night? We could still catch a movie . . . or rent one?"

She pressed the light button on her wristwatch. "Brody's picking me up at eleven. I've got choir practice at nine tomorrow morning. . . ."

"I'll get you there on time."

She looked at me skeptically, as we've been known to talk all night.

"C'mon!"

"Okay. But I've got to interview the DJ first. It shouldn't take long. You want to meet me back here in fifteen minutes?"

I shrugged. "Sure."

But after five minutes of watching glow sticks bob and waiting for Adrienne to return, I began feeling very self-conscious. My hands were suddenly odd and awkward attachments that didn't seem to belong anywhere. Then I realized that light from the locker room was shining on me. It began to feel like a spotlight. A spotlight on a dweeby wallflower with odd and awkward hands hanging out by the girls' locker room.

I finally moved toward the dark safety of the bleachers. I sat on the edge of the first row, alone, keeping an eye on the place Adrienne said she'd meet me.

Blake Jennings walked by with his arm around a girl.

She looked like a freshman.

I couldn't tell if her ears were wet or dry.

A few minutes later Sunshine Holden staggered by, possibly drunk, definitely crying.

Stu Dillard was nowhere in sight.

The bleacher seats behind me started thumping and shaking, and when I turned around, I saw Eddie Pasco coming toward me.

Eddie Pasco is Larkmont's soccer star. He foots a ball everywhere. Between classes, at lunch, after school, around the track, on the cross-country course . . . he and his soccer ball are inseparable. One of his girlfriends Magic Markered big eyes and oversized lips on his soccer ball and wrote "Eddie's True Love" when she dumped him. Everyone agrees it's one of Larkmont High's best breakups.

Eddie Pasco is also in my psychology class. He sits in the back fantasizing about soccer, much to Mr. Stills's obvious annoyance.

"I've never seen you at a dance before," Eddie said, sitting beside me.

"I'm not big on school dances," I confirmed.

"But here you are," he said, a twinkle in his eye.

I snorted. "I must be insane."

"Rumor has it," he said with a nod.

"Hey!" I backhanded him. "Not nice!"

He laughed. "So who you with?"

"Nobody." I eyed him. "You with the soccer ball?"

He gave me a very appealing, very seductive grin. "Not nice."

I shrugged, but I could feel myself blushing.

He maintained the sexy grin. "Feel like dancing?"

The memory of a soggy ear clouded my mind. "It depends," I said, scrutinizing him, "on what kind of kisser you are."

His grin grew broader. "Isn't that a little backward?"

"I'm not going out there so you can maul my ear," I said firmly. "I've had enough ear mauling for one night."

"Your ears are not what interest me," he said. Then he cupped his hand behind my head and pulled our faces together.

41

Wasted Breath

EDDIE PASCO TASTED LIKE BEER. And spicy wings. With traces of burned or charred . . . something. The taste, the *odor,* was very distracting. Familiar, but not.

What *was* it?

Where had I smelled it before?

In . . . the bathrooms?

As my senses finally connected the dots, I pulled away from him, mentally slapping myself upside the head. Eddie Pasco was stoned!

"Hey! Where you going?" he asked, pulling me back.

"Uh . . . you're wasted?" I said, trying to free myself.

A disarming grin crossed his face. "Aw c'mon. I had, like, one beer and a coupla hits. That's it."

I broke away and said, "Sorry, I'm just not into that," but I felt oddly conflicted. I didn't want to be with a guy who drank beer and smoked pot, yet I'd basically asked a stoner to kiss me.

And the real killer was . . . it hadn't been a muddled gray kiss, or a barely pink one.

It had shot past crimson to fiery red.

42

Flashbacks

BRODY WAS ALREADY WAITING in the parking lot when we finally got out of the gym, so Adrienne begged off spending the night and I didn't put up much of a fight. I was still muddled over Eddie.

Adrienne hadn't seen the kiss, and I wasn't sure I wanted to tell her about it. I certainly wasn't going to spill it in front of Brody! (There are some things you just don't discuss in front of brothers, be they blood or adopted.)

So while Adrienne chatted about her interview with the DJ, I searched the radio for some decent rock 'n' roll to block out the residual tingles from Eddie Pasco's red-hot kiss. Nothing seemed to work, though. His kiss was like a forbidden flashback that I couldn't seem to block from my mind.

I was dropped off at the condo at 10:58, only to discover that my mom was not home.

"Dessert and coffee," I mocked. "Dessert and coffee, that's all."

I devoured rocky road right out of the carton, trying to cool the sizzle of Eddie's kiss.

Bite after bite just melted.

At 11:37 I finally put away the carton, washed off my makeup, and went to bed. I wasn't even close to sleeping when the digits on my clock said 12:02 and the muted jangle of bracelets and keys announced Mom's return.

"Have a good time?" I called. "You think maybe he's the one?"

She came into my room. "Please don't be like that. Your father and I had a lot to discuss."

Even in the dim light from the hallway, I could see she was dressed in a way I hadn't seen in a long time: fitted leather jacket, tight jeans, stylish boots . . . just my dad's style.

I pulled the covers over my shoulder and turned my back.

She continued: "I would have called, but I was afraid of waking you up. . . ."

I flipped around and sat up. "How can you talk to him? How can you trust him? You know what he's capable of!"

"I'm not naïve, Evangeline. But we were married for eighteen years. We have a lot of history, a lot of memories. It's very hard to let it all go."

I flopped back down. Let them have their history. Let them have their memories. I didn't want to think about him or her or what used to be.

I had a memory of my own that was refusing to go away.

43

Disconnection

My dad called too early the next morning. (Okay, it was ten o'clock, but any time before noon on a Saturday is too early.) I knew it was him because I could hear my mother's side of the conversation:

"No, it's fine, I was up."

(The liar.)

"That's interesting. . . ."

(Yeah, I'll bet.)

"No, I don't think that's a good idea."

(Finally! She's come to her senses.)

"I'll tell her."

(Wait. *Her?* Who? *Me?*)

"What was his name again?"

(His name? Whose name?)

"He must've just gotten it out of the phone book."

(Someone—some *guy*—was trying to reach me? Who?)

I suffered through a very long pause; then my mother's voice started up again. "*You* may think it's a good opportunity, Jon, but I know she'll just hang up on you. I'll give her the information."

She sounded so firm. So in control. So uncharacteristically *calm*.

But after another pause, something began churning under the calm. "Jon, she's *not* dating," she whispered. "I would know, wouldn't I? And so what if she was? Are you forgetting that she's almost seventeen?"

(Yeah!)

"And why would he call *your* house? She would have given him *our* number!"

(Score one for logic!)

Then in a loud, testy tone she said, "Jon, stop! You are in no position to screen her boyfriends!"

(Boyfriends?)

"No, *you* listen to *me*. Stop being so controlling!"

When she hung up, I emerged from my bedroom and said, "That was tellin' him, Mom." I meant it, too.

She closed her eyes, and I could see that she was trying to collect herself, but her face stayed flushed, her nostrils flared. And after presumably reaching the calming number of ten, she shoved the phone notepad toward me. "As I'm sure you overheard, you had a call." She studied me. "Is this someone we should know about?"

"We?" I asked with an eyebrow suitably cocked.

"I. Is this someone *I* should know about?"

I read what was scrawled on the notepad and tried to act nonchalant as I said, "Just someone in my math class. Probably needs help with homework."

There was no *way* I was going to tell her about Robbie Marshall.

44

Waving a Plastic Spade

OVER THE WEEKEND I made a valiant attempt to focus on my schoolwork. I also did heaps of laundry, organized my dresser, listened to Jet's *Get Born* at supersonic volume, and spent Sunday afternoon at the Willows'.

I most definitely did *not* call Robbie Marshall.

Being at the Willows' was just like old times. Adrienne's parents were out back on their patio, enjoying the beautiful weather as they read through the Sunday paper and thumbed through stacks of catalogs.

Brody, Adrienne, and I wound up in the garage, blasting music and playing cutthroat Ping-Pong. We compete for the "golden paddle," which is just a paddle that was sprayed gold years ago (and has very little gold left on it). I'm a pretty slammin' player when there's a rockin' song on, which is why Adrienne's always messing with the station between points when I'm beating her. She knows that rap, synth, or pop will throw me off, and is not afraid to use this. Brody seems to thrive on rock, too, so he just fights back harder, which I like.

It occurred to me that Adrienne didn't know about Eddie's kiss, or Andrew's kiss, or about Robbie calling, or even that he'd asked me out. But the afternoon went by and I didn't catch her up. I just wanted to enjoy some uncomplicated time at the Willows', with things like they used to be before I moved.

On my walk home, I must have been in a good-old-days state of mind, because I accidentally went past my old house. Ever since we'd moved out, I'd taken a roundabout route to Adrienne's just to avoid seeing the house. For some reason, I just couldn't take seeing it.

I think Mom felt the same way, which is why *we* moved out when, really, my dad should have.

I did go back once early on, to retrieve my iPod and a big box of CDs, which had somehow not made it in the move. I was also planning to snatch the computer. Why should my dad get it? He mostly just surfed the Web and used it for e-mailing gig announcements, whereas I desperately needed it for school.

But when I arrived, there was a FOR SALE sign dangling from a four-by-four post.

My home. My childhood. Up for sale.

I'd stood by the hedge of hibiscus shrubs that lined our property and stared at the sign. And after a while I'd become aware of how tall the hibiscus plants were. When had that happened? They were taller than I was. And the blooms were amazing. Together the shrubs made a beautiful living fence of alternating reds, yellows, and pinks.

Pictures of me as a toddler waving a plastic spade as Mom planted hibiscus shrubs had flashed through my mind. They were small plants then; baby bushes with just a smattering of leaves, shivering in the wind, yards apart. I could have crushed them with one mighty stomp of my toddler foot.

As the FOR SALE sign clinked in the afternoon breeze that day, it had struck me how ironic it was that the bushes were now large and bursting with blooms, while I felt small and vulnerable.

I hadn't retrieved my iPod or CDs, or the computer; I'd gone back to the condo and cried. And after that I'd never returned. Why torture yourself when you don't have to?

But I must've had a brain fade when I left Adrienne's, because I suddenly found myself approaching the hibiscus hedge.

I could still have turned around without actually seeing the house, but I told myself that would be ridiculous. I had moved on! I was no longer living in the past! I had places to go! People to kiss! Fantasies to live!

So I went forward, and the first thing I noticed was that the FOR SALE sign was missing.

I was gripped with a sudden and crippling fear.

Had the house been sold?

Why hadn't they told me?

But fear turned to shock when I spotted my mother's car parked beside my dad's in the driveway.

It was so strange to see them there. The same cars that had been parked alongside each other every evening for years. Her Toyota. His '65 Mustang.

I tried to convince myself that their cars being parked together didn't mean my *parents* were parked together. Maybe she was strong enough now, *brave* enough now to face the memories. Maybe she had to talk to him there to finish closing the hole he'd blasted in her heart.

I considered going up to the door.

But . . . what would I do? Knock? Walk right in?

And what would I say?

"I'm home!"?

It was all so ridiculous.

There was no going back.

45

Ghosts

Delilah threw herself upon her sister's gravesite and wept. Her exit from the house had been witnessed by no one, so at last she was free to let the long-held torrent of tears escape. Why Elise? her heart wailed. Why Elise? She had been so young, so innocent, so good. The question echoed madly in Delilah's mind as her body convulsed with the pain of her loss. Try as she would, she could find no justifiable answer.

Between the house and the condo there's a small graveyard. It's off the main road, through a little wooded area, and it's very old-timey. The statues are crooked and mossy, the surrounding trees have large, knotty branches dragged low by ivy, and the grounds are completely overgrown. I'm sure no one new has been buried there for at least a hundred years.

It's the classic scream-inducing graveyard, and Adrienne and I used to go by it on our way home from school for a rush. At first it was just "Climb the fence—I dare you!" Then it was "Touch the headstone—I dare you!" Gradually we got deeper and deeper into the graveyard, and finally (on the first of October in our fifth-grade year), we made it all the way to the four-casket crypt in the middle of spooksville.

We were gutsy girls!

I hadn't been there in years, but somehow I wound up there now.

I didn't throw myself on any graves and cry. I didn't cry at all. Why would I? No one I knew was dead. No, I just walked, which was actually very pleasant, very serene. I could hear cars in the distance, but barely. Birds twittered, butterflies fluttered, and there was a soothing rustle of leaves in the early-evening breeze. I was actually enjoying myself until I realized that I was doing something I'd never done before:

I was reading the names on the tombstones.

It was eerie and unnerving, not because these people were once alive and were now *dead,* but because I was searching for a particular name.

Elise.

"Why are you doing this?" I muttered to myself, but I couldn't seem to stop. "You're insane!" I said between clenched teeth. "She's not real. She's *not real.*"

The growing darkness was what finally sent me home. The darkness and the chill and the uneasy feeling that none of it was real. Maybe the story *and* the passion were all just fantasy.

Maybe there was no such thing as a crimson kiss.

I looked behind me several times as I hurried out of the graveyard, and after I was through the gate, I ran. Arms pumping, lungs burning, feet flying, I *ran.*

When I reached the condo, I tried to compose myself, but my heart was still pounding madly as I stepped through the door.

"There you are!" my mom cried. "I was worried. Adrienne said you left her house hours ago!"

Had it been hours?

I stopped trying to restrain my panting. "I needed some exercise."

"Some exercise? For hours? In blue jeans and a knit top?"

I gave what I hoped was a disarming laugh. "It was so nice out. I walked for miles!"

How could I tell her I'd spent the evening walking through a cemetery alone, searching for something that didn't exist?

I couldn't even explain it to myself.

46

Heavy-Metal Kissing

APPARENTLY ROBBIE MARSHALL GETS ANNOYED when he's ignored. He was already lurking in the vicinity of math class when I arrived on campus Monday morning, and before I could slip by him, he grabbed me by the arm and said, "Why didn't you call me back?"

I pulled a face. "Is there a law that says I have to?"

"When someone calls you four times, yeah. There's a law."

I yanked my arm free. "There should be a law against calling someone four times!"

Hurt crinkled his eyes. "Am I really that bad a kisser?"

In an instant, my brain mapped out the delivery route of this news: I'd made a snotty remark to Sunshine at the dance, Stu had heard; one of the two of them had delivered it back to Robbie.

Probably Sunshine.

Was there no honor among jilted lovers?

Aw, who was I fooling? I was an idiot to have ever made the

remark. It was catty, and I should have known it would get back to Robbie.

I let out a sigh. "Look, I'm sorry. Obviously lots of girls think you're a great kisser."

"But you don't," he said, still crinkly-eyed.

"Forget me. What do I know? Think of Sunshine or Jasmine or Nicole." I swept my hands upward. "Anyone, really." I laughed. "I'm sure you have no problem finding compatible kissers."

"But I thought *we* were compatible." His head bobbed. "I thought we were *really* compatible!"

"Hmm." I screwed my mouth to the side, wondering how best to explain this. "I think I'm a classical or blues kisser, whereas you are definitely heavy metal."

He stared at me, his eyebrows knitting. "So you're what? A Mozart kisser? And I'm, like, Metallica?"

I laughed, "You're more like Slipknot." I started toward the classroom, saying, "There are plenty of heavy-metal chicks out there, Robbie. I'm just not one of them."

"Wait!" he said, catching up to me. "So what's a Mozart kiss like?"

I hesitated, because for some reason this impressed me. Why'd he even care? If there was one thing I was certain of, it was that Robbie Marshall had no interest in classical music. And to be fair, my education in classical music is pretty limited, too. So I said, "Actually, I'm more Stevie Ray Vaughn than Mozart."

"Who?"

"Blues guitarist? Wrote 'Crossfire,' 'Texas Flood,' 'Life Without You'? Died tragically in a plane crash in the prime of his life?"

"Oh, oh, yeah, right," he said, obviously clueless about Stevie

Y--9090

Mitchell Park

ex Wed Nov 02 2022

barcode: 31185014373213
Title: Confessions of a serial kisser / Wendelin

Sat Oct 22 2022 10:51AM

Ray or his music. But why would he know about some blues guitarist who died before we were even born?

Why did I?

Again my brain mapped out the routing, and it sent a painful jolt through me when I found myself face to face with my dad. Him and the worn acoustic guitar he kept in the living room. Him strumming, picking, playing Eric Clapton, Bruce Springsteen, and Stevie Ray Vaughn, singing softly, hoarsely, behind the quivering strings.

"What's that?" I'd asked him the first time he'd played "Life Without You," when I was about nine.

"A little number by Stevie Ray," he'd told me. Then he'd sung it for me from the beginning.

When he was done, I clapped like I always did. He gave a grand bow with his guitar like he always did, and then I said what I'd been thinking: "It sounds like that 'Little Wing' song you play. By that Jimi guy?"

He stared at me a moment, then swept the guitar off over his head and scooped me up in his arms. "You're a genius, angel! An absolute genius!"

"I am?" I giggled.

"Stevie Ray Vaughn was really influenced by Jimi Hendrix. The song I just played is a great example of that!" He turned and called, "Lorena! Honey! Our angel is a musical genius!"

At that moment the world was a happy, perfect place.

"So what's a Stevie Ray . . . Von kiss like?" Robbie was asking.

I shook my head and walked past him. "Forget Stevie Ray," I choked out. "Stevie Ray is dead."

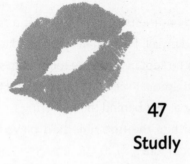

47
Studly

THE INTENSIVE ACADEMIC RETRACKING I'D DONE over the weekend didn't do me a bit of good. I was a basket case through math, a space case through history, I couldn't find Adrienne at break, and afterward Spanish and American lit were just a blur. By lunchtime I didn't even want to find Adrienne. I just wanted to be left alone.

Unfortunately, Stu Dillard had other plans. "Hey, gorgeous, hold up!" he called as I meandered toward the outskirts of campus.

I scowled at him. "Since when am I 'gorgeous,' huh, Studly?"

He draped an arm over my shoulders and gave me a very disarming smile. "I think you've probably always been. I was just too dumb to notice."

"Nice," I said, giving him a little smile back. It was the first time I'd smiled all day, but this was Studly I was dealing with, so I didn't let myself feel too amused by his comment. Instead, I changed the subject. "So where's Sunshine?"

"Sunshine?" He nodded thoughtfully. "The Dark Cloud of Lark-mont High has her covered."

I squinted at him. "Huh?"

He laughed. "Hey, come on. I'm trying to be clever and literary here to appeal to your intellect."

I squinted even harder. Studly trying to be clever and literary was quite a stretch, never mind his wanting to appeal to someone's *intellect*.

And yet . . . he'd said it with such off-the-cuff ease that it seemed almost possible.

He snorted. "Look. All she does is cry about Robbie. I'm not into mopping up someone else's mess."

As we walked along, his arm moved with a sweeping confidence from my shoulders to my waist. I shook my head. "You can just forget it, Studly. You have hippity-hopped yourself right out of my affections."

One dark eyebrow arched high. "You're referring to the amusing comment I tossed your way?"

"You didn't 'toss' it, you shouted it. And quit trying to sound smart! I'm beginning to feel like you're mocking me."

He swept me around to face him. "I'm not stupid, Evangeline, and I'm just trying to figure you out."

"Figure me out? *Why?*"

He gave me a coy smile. "I find the change in you intriguing."

I slapped his chest. "Stop talking like that!"

"Does it make you trepidatious?"

"Trepidatious? Stop it!" I squinted at him. "Is that even a word?"

He laughed, then said, "I have a theory about you."

"A *theory* about me? I don't want you to have a *theory* about me!

Just ignore me, okay? Forget I exist. Treat me like you did a month ago!"

He ignored me, all right. "My *theory* is that you, Evangeline Bianca Logan, are looking for a perfect kiss."

I froze. How did he know my middle name?

How had he figured this out?

He pulled me closer, his grasp firm but not forceful. "Robbie, Justin, Andrew, Blake, Eddie, plus some random dude at Starbucks, and probably a few more that I haven't heard about ... You're looking for something, Evangeline, and I think I might have it."

His breath was warm and laced with spearmint. I'd never noticed his lips before, but now that's all I saw. "I didn't kiss Blake," I protested. "He licked my ear. That doesn't count...."

His mouth was against mine now, brushing softly, with gentle almost-kisses. "You're right," he whispered. "That's no way to kiss a goddess."

A goddess?

I felt myself melting in his arms as he pulled me closer to show me how it *was* done.

It was, without a doubt, a wonderfully executed kiss. And as it grew deeper, I couldn't help kissing him back, waiting to be filled with the transcendent magic of a crimson kiss.

I waited...

And waited...

But nothing happened.

Nothing.

48

Quarterback Sneak

It didn't help that Stu wanted a kiss analysis.

"On a scale of one to ten, what would you give it?"

"Oh, please!"

"Aw, come on. Admit it—it was a ten!"

I shook my head. "I'm not doing that, Stu." Then I added, "But I will say you have lovely execution and style."

"Aha!" he cawed. "Better than Robbie, right?"

That was a no-brainer, but I said, "It's not a competition."

And *that's* when I realized that yes, of course it was. Stu was a tier beneath Robbie on the hotness scale, a tier beneath him on the jock scale, and, consequently, a tier beneath him on the babe-magnet scale. Beating him at something, *anything* (besides academics, of course), was the key to the happiness of his male ego.

Still, I didn't feel right turning over that key. He'd called me a goddess, but he was treating me like a scorekeeper! So I said, "Sorry to break it to you, Stu, but kissing is not a sport."

"Sure it is," he said with a grin. "It's a contact sport!"

I laughed, because on the scale of witty remarks he had it all over Robbie.

"So where are we in the game?" he asked as he grabbed my hand and pulled me in. "It's at least first down, right? I think it's time to make another pass."

I wrestled free from him. "Sorry, Stu, but I'm going to blow the whistle right here."

"You're benching me?"

He was giving me an exaggerated pout, which was somehow very . . . disarming, but then I noticed that we were being watched. "We've got company," I said, nodding in Sunshine's direction.

"Aw, *maaaaan*," he groaned when he saw her.

Those two words did not translate to, Oh, bother, we broke up and she's stalking me. No, he'd pulled a sneak play! Sunshine obviously had no idea that Stu resented mopping up Robbie's mess, or that he saw himself as a free agent, able to play ball wherever he wanted. Sunshine thought she had an exclusive contract, and she was not planning to release Stu anytime soon.

"You are so bad," I said with a snort. "Try to remember whose team you're on, will you?" Then, to save him further awkwardness or embarrassment, I gave him a friendly punch in the arm and walked off.

During chemistry I tried not to think about Stu or his unsettling knowledge of my kissing history. I also tried not to think about how his beautifully executed kiss had left me cold. I tried really hard not to ask, What is *wrong* with me?

Instead, I focused on Mr. Kiraly. And although it's easy to lose the content of the lesson while watching Mr. Kiraly's middle fingers do their thing, I did not let my mind drift. I focused on his words. Electrolysis of water, hydrogen forming at the cathode, oxygen forming at the anode . . . now *that* made sense.

Then I went to psychology, and as I sat down, it struck me that I'd kissed *two* sets of lips in this class. Andrew "Let Me Say You're Welcome" Prescott and Eddie "It's Not Your Ears That Interest Me" Pasco.

Two out of . . . twelve (counting guys only, of course).

That was one-sixth of the class kissed.

Point one-six-six-six-six-six of the class kissed.

Three would make it a quarter!

Four would make it a third!

At six I'd be up to half!

I looked around at the ten other kissing prospects and accidentally caught Andrew's eye.

He gave me an awkward wave. A puppy-dog look.

I waved back and quickly turned away.

Then Eddie Pasco walked in tardy, and the memory of his kiss sent a hot flush through my body and up to my cheeks.

With a grin, Eddie and his soccer ball passed by my desk. "Wanna dance?" he murmured, then took his seat in the back of the classroom.

I sat up stiffly and faced forward, not daring to glance back.

Mr. Stills took roll, then heaved a heavy sigh and began his last lecture of the day. Sigmund Freud was the subject, the irony being that Mr. Stills's dour delivery made us all long for a couch to lie down on.

But couches aren't standard issue at Larkmont High, and Eddie had totally broken the concentration I'd mustered in chemistry. My mind instead drifted (as it so often did) to a passage from *A Crimson Kiss*. I was looking alert, following Mr. Stills as he moved back and forth, but I have very little recollection of what he said. All I heard was the passage, running endlessly through my head.

> *She ached for him. It was a new sensation, unbridled now by the sight of him. His dancing eyes, framed by jet-black brows; the lock of hair that fell defiantly over his forehead; the presence of taut, lean muscles, flexing under the crisp lines of his shirt.*
>
> *And his voice.*
>
> *His husky, lilting voice.*
>
> *These things combined and combusted in Delilah's heart, turning to ash the quiet numbness that had engulfed her for so long.*

When the dismissal bell rang, I grabbed my things and bolted for the door without so much as a glance behind me.

Eddie Pasco was not my Grayson.

Eddie Pasco was a stoner!

I needed to find someone else.

I needed to find a real crimson kiss!

49

Tongue-Twisted

I CAUGHT UP WITH ADRIENNE in the parking lot. "Can I come over?" I asked, panting heavily from having run the obstacle course that is the student parking lot.

She hesitated as she opened the passenger door of Brody's truck. "I've got exactly an hour and a half before I've got to be back here for choir. And I've got a ton of homework."

I frowned. "Darn."

"Something up?" she asked.

I stepped away from the truck. I needed to *talk* to her, not rush through telling her about everything that had happened. "You know what? I'll just catch up with you tomorrow."

Brody called, "Hey, at least let us give you a ride home!"

So I scooted in and gave him a halfhearted "Hey, Chevy-man!"

"Cool boots," he said, eyeing my feet as he fired up the truck.

"My mom's," I answered. Then I exchanged looks with Adrienne and asked Brody, "So . . . do you like boots on a girl?"

He shrugged, navigating his way into the lineup of cars waiting to blast their way to freedom. "I don't know. I guess. They look good on you."

I shrugged in Adrienne's direction and settled in. "Well, thanks."

"Oh!" Adrienne said, obviously remembering something of extreme importance. "Paxton says tutoring's in Room Two Twelve on Tuesdays and Thursdays. You can start anytime."

I groaned. "I forgot all about that."

Brody chuckled, then fired off, "Tutoring's in Two Twelve on Tuesdays and Thursdays," like it was some tongue twister rather than the torture I was going to have to endure for who knew how many afternoons.

Adrienne leaned forward, facing him as she said it even faster. "Tutoring's in Two Twelve on Tuesdays and Thursdays!"

"Tutoring's in Two Twelve on Tuesdays and Thursdays!" he countered, his tongue tap-dancing across the syllables.

"Tutoring's in Two Twelve on Tuesdays and Thursdays!" Adrienne shouted.

"Tutoring's in Two Twelve on Tuesdays and Thursdays!" Brody fired back.

"Tutoring's—"

"Stop!" I cried, covering my ears.

There was a heartbeat of silence; then Brody murmured, "As you wish," and turned into traffic.

As I wish? I gave Brody a questioning look, but his focus was on traffic, not me. So I turned to Adrienne to get some reassurance that I hadn't been out of line, but her focus wasn't on me, either. She was staring at her brother, her mouth slightly agape.

Okay. So I wasn't the only one who thought Brody's comment

was odd. But when we got on Larkmont Boulevard, Brody turned on the radio—which has always been my job.

"Oh, I love this song!" Adrienne said, cranking it up. And that was the end of any conversation. Before I knew it, they were dropping me off.

50

Intersection

THAT NIGHT, as Mom and I were enjoying a perfectly pleasant bowl of double-fudge ice cream, she brought up the subject of my dad, trying to convince me that "we should get together as a family and talk."

I, in turn, told her that "we should get together as a family and hammer nails into each other." I frowned at her. "It would definitely be more fun."

"Look, sweetheart," she said, scraping daintily at her ice cream, "your birthday's coming up and—"

"And what? You'd like to ruin it by inviting *him*?" I dug up a glacier of ice cream and bit in. "No thank you!"

"You and he used to be so close . . ."

"Stop it! The past is *behind* us. It's *over*. Why are you letting yourself be manipulated by him? Whose idea was it for you to go over to the house, huh? His, right?"

She blinked at me a moment, realizing that I was fully aware of her little rendezvous. Finally she took a deep breath and said, "Look. I really think we should all go to counseling together. We can get things out and an objective third party can help us sort through our feelings."

I shoved back from the table. "You can go. I don't need a third party—I know exactly how I feel." I folded my napkin and restated the obvious: "My father's a two-timing jerk and I don't want to see him."

She gave me a pitiful look. "But he's sorry, honey. He's really, truly sorry."

"He should be," I told her, and went to bed.

In the morning, I was half awakened by tingling. Tingling, and a racing heart. I hugged my feather pillow close. It was a warm, soft cloud, and I sank into it deeper and deeper.

"Aaah!" I cried, jolting upright.

I'd been dreaming about Eddie Pasco.

I threw back the covers and got out of bed, muttering, "Don't be insane!"

I showered and blew out my hair, and with half an hour to spare after dressing and putting on my makeup, I decided I deserved a frappuccino for breakfast.

A grande!

With whipped cream!

Unfortunately, my dad was parked outside the condo when I slipped out the door.

I walked past him and his ridiculously cool Mustang.

He got out and followed me.

"Evangeline! Evangeline, please. Talk to me."

I kept walking.

"Evangeline, come on. How many times and ways do I have to say I'm sorry. I was a jackass. Yes, I know. Yes, you're right."

The light at the intersection was green, so I stepped into the crosswalk with great confidence, ignoring him. And then my shoe started squeaking.

Why was my shoe squeaking?

Why did today of all days have to be squeaky shoe day?

"Angel, please!"

I spun on him. "Don't you ever, *ever* call me that again," I seethed.

Then I ran away, leaving him in the middle of the intersection with traffic idling in all directions.

51

Bumping into Tatiana

WHEN I GOT TO SCHOOL, I took my frappuccino directly to Room 212 and signed up for after-school tutoring.

"When can you start?" the teacher asked after she saw that I'd checked off math and chemistry as areas of strength. "We're desperate for chemistry and math tutors."

"Today," I answered.

"Wonderful!" She put out her hand. "I'm Mrs. Huffington. Delighted to have you on board, Evangeline."

I shook hands and left, and immediately ran into Tatiana Phillips.

"Evangeline?" She blushed. "Wow. You look really . . . different."

I couldn't seem to find any words.

"I . . . I'm sorry you didn't come out for volleyball this year."

"Not your fault," I managed.

"Thanks," she said, and she seemed relieved. Not in a phony, dramatic way. More like she'd been secretly holding her breath and could finally let it go. "I'm sorry," she said, looking down, "about everything."

I nodded. "The whole thing stinks."

"You're telling me." She glanced at me. "Is your mom taking him back?"

I don't know why, but I rolled my eyes and gave a goofy smirk. "I sure hope not."

She laughed. "Parents, huh?"

I laughed, too. "Exactly."

"We missed you on the team this year," she said, and her eyes looked soft and a little sad.

I snorted. "Oh, right. You missed me all the way to league championship!" Then I added, "Congratulations, by the way."

She nodded. "Thanks." Then suddenly she shot forward and gave me a hug. "Please come out next year," she whispered.

All at once my chin quivered, my eyes stung, and my throat totally closed up.

I couldn't speak, but I could still nod, and I could hug her back.

So that's what I did.

52

An Unexpected Kindness

ROBBIE MARSHALL WAS STANDING OUTSIDE OF MATH when I arrived. It being Tuesday, I couldn't help but notice his pumped-up arms. Biceps the size of softballs, triceps like fleshy mountain ridges.

He was, without question, sizzling hot.

He tugged out his earbuds when he saw me coming and pressed off his iPod. "I downloaded some Stevie Ray last night. He's awesome!"

I stopped cold. All of a sudden I was back in the intersection with my father. All of a sudden coffee for breakfast didn't feel like such a good idea. All of a sudden I was just *shaky*.

"Evangeline?" Robbie asked, stepping forward.

"Please," I said weakly. "Please don't ever mention Stevie Ray Vaughn again."

"But—"

"I'm sorry. I know it doesn't make sense."

He looked crushed, and I felt bad, but I wasn't about to explain.

Robbie followed me inside and took his seat, too, but I avoided looking at him. As other people filed in, I went through the motions of preparing for class. Planner out. Homework out. Pencil out. Book out. Then I tried to look busy, even though I had nothing left to do.

"Psst!"

It was Robbie, leaning across Sandra Herrera's desk.

I shook my head and didn't look over.

"Pssssst!" he said louder.

How annoying did he want to be?

I flashed him an angry look, which softened immediately when I saw that he was trying to give me something.

A small, crisp, white paper sack.

"I got these for you," he whispered.

I probably should have refused the gift, but it's hard not to take something that's being held out to you.

So I took the sack.

There was a box inside.

A little white cardboard box.

I gave him a puzzled look.

Robbie Marshall may have arms of steel and diamond-encrusted teeth, but the smile that danced across his face was boyish and very shy. "Open it."

Sandra Herrera appeared as the tardy bell rang, putting a human screen between us. And as Mrs. Fieldman clapped her hands and called, "Settle down—we've got lots to cover today!" I peeked inside the little white box.

Robbie Marshall had brought me chocolates.

53

Avoiding Sweets

"HE BROUGHT YOU *CHOCOLATES*?" Adrienne gasped when I showed them to her at break.

"I tried to give them back, but he wouldn't take them."

"Are you going to go out with him?"

I shook my head.

"Are you going to *eat* them?" she asked, staring at the box.

I shook my head again. "I'm not sure."

"I'll help you," she offered, a mischievous grin dancing across her face.

They were still unopened at lunchtime, unlike the gossip circuit. Word had been transmitted to Sunshine, who found me in the Snack Shack line and immediately began short-circuiting. "I just want to know if it's true," she said, her eyes sparking.

"Probably not," I replied. "Especially if you heard it at school."

"Quit being clever and just tell me!" She glanced over her

shoulder, one way, then the other. "If he brought you chocolates, I'm going to kill him!"

I moved forward with the line. "Then he most definitely did not bring me chocolates."

"He did, didn't he! You're not going, 'Chocolates? What chocolates?' You know exactly what I'm talking about!"

I sighed and said, "Look, Sunshine. Robbie and I are not going out. Stu and I are not going out. You can have either of them or both of them. I don't care."

For some reason, this totally popped her fuse. "He never brought *me* chocolates. Ever. And I did a lot more to deserve them than you!"

I resisted the obvious and very tempting retort and instead said, "Can you take it up with him? Because this conversation is making me lose my appetite, and I've really been looking forward to a half-frozen bean burrito all day."

She took a step back and stared at me. "You are *weird*. Just *weird*."

I nodded. "Well. I'm glad we've cleared that up."

She made a strangled-sounding noise and stormed off.

After I bought lunch, I set off to find Adrienne, but in the process I ran into Eddie Pasco.

"Hey," he said, looking at me with bedroom eyes. "I had a dream about you last night."

"Aaah!" I cried, bolting past him.

With a laugh, he followed me, footing his soccer ball along as he went. "It was a great dream. . . ."

"I don't want to hear about it!"

"Sure you do."

"No! I don't!"

Trevor Dansa was coming toward us. Trevor Dansa with the khaki Dockers, polo shirt, and 4.0. Trevor Dansa, whom I'd known since seventh grade, whom I'd done science fair projects and PowerPoint presentations with. Conservative, *sober,* and moderately handsome Trevor Dansa.

Eddie was grinning at me as his feet spun and toed and caressed his soccer ball. "There was honey involved." One eyebrow arched in my direction. "Do you like honey?"

That was it. I didn't want to imagine him and me and honey! And I should probably have run or ducked into the girls' bathroom, but instead I grabbed Trevor Dansa by his polo shirt buttons . . . and kissed him.

54

The Pitfalls of Avoidance

NEVER SURPRISE-KISS A BOY who's listening to an iPod. (Unfortunately, in my rush to get away from Eddie, I hadn't noticed the earbuds.)

Trevor's lips were a confused knot as he yanked the buds out of his ears. "What are you doing?" he mumbled into my mouth.

"Just kiss me!" I demanded.

So he did. Or, at least, he tried to.

Let's just say he's better at PowerPoint.

But still, to my great relief Eddie Pasco and his soccer ball did move on, leaving me with a very awkward Trevor Dansa. "Thank you for saving me," I said. "He was stalking me."

"Eddie was?" he asked.

I nodded. "He had some dream about me and honey. I didn't want to hear it."

Trevor blinked at me, then blushed.

"So thanks," I said, backing away from him. "You're a lifesaver."

"Sure," he kind of stammered.

I continued my search for Adrienne but never did find her. She wasn't in the Performance Pavilion like she said she would be, and the choir classroom was locked up tight. So I sat on the walkway in an isolated corner of the 400 block and picked at my cold burrito, vowing to start packing my own lunches. I was craving lettuce and tomatoes. Sliced turkey. Whole wheat bread!

"Evangeline?"

It was the literature lover herself, carrying an armful of library books. "Hi, Miss Ryder."

"What are you doing here ... all by yourself ... on cement ...?" she asked, peering at me through her black rectangular glasses. It struck me that even her regular speech was stylized. She seemed to dance with words, waltzing with them through the unexpected twists and turns of life.

"Eating a sucky burrito," I so eloquently replied.

She smiled at me. "Sounds appetizing . . . in a school cafeteria kind of way."

I gave a wry nod. "Exactly."

Having exhausted the subject of my delectable lunch, you'd think Miss Ryder would have moved on. Instead, she asked, "So what are you reading?"

I didn't have a book in my hands. I had a burrito.

She smiled when she saw my expression. "For pleasure! What book are you reading for pleasure?"

I grimaced. "Not *The Last of the Mohicans,* that's for sure."

She laughed. "Perhaps you'd like some recommendations?" She started fingering the spines of her books, reading the titles aloud.

I stopped her with a gentle "That's okay, Miss Ryder."

"Are you sure?" She smiled demurely. "Sucky burritos taste a lot better with a good book."

"Actually, I do have one." I opened my book bag and showed her the tattered pages of *A Crimson Kiss,* being careful not to reveal the cover.

"Oh, very good!" she said, then moved away, saying, "Friends may fail you, but books never do."

I watched her go, thinking about what she'd said.

Then I put my burrito aside and opened my book. Didn't matter what page. Anywhere was good. I just dived in and escaped.

55

Page 143

"WAIT!" SHE CRIED, *then immediately softened the command with a plaintive plea. "Don't go."*

Silence fell in the wake of her words. At every turn this maddening woman rebuffed him. Why should he stay?

But Grayson found himself drawn in again by her haunted eyes. He longed to help her surface from the depths of her agony, not just for gasps of air but for full, deep breaths of life's sweetness. Time and time again he'd pulled her up, only to watch her submerge once more into her dark sea of unnavigable despair.

Silently he cursed himself. How could he liberate her from the past when she held so tightly to it? Was it not wiser to walk through the door now than endure another inevitable round of defeat?

With a determined air, Grayson turned his back and strode toward the door.

"Please" came her hoarse, desperate whisper.

He turned to face her.

"Please," she whispered again.

It was all he needed.

56

Tutoring

To my great relief, Eddie Pasco ignored me in psychology.

If only Andrew Prescott had done the same.

Instead, I had to endure his dejected puppy-dog look and quivery smile. Even though I only saw it for the fleeting moment I dared a look in his direction, it was seared into my brain for the rest of the class period. It reminded me of a ripped-out hangnail (which, for some reason, I had a few of).

When the dismissal bell rang, I bolted out of the classroom, wondering how my quest for a kiss had gone so terribly wrong. I felt uncomfortable everywhere, and in my hurry to get away from Eddie and Andrew, I was actually *early* to tutoring.

Now I felt dweeby, too!

So I sauntered around a little, then returned to the infamous Room 212.

A girl with short, bleached hair, Paxton, and Mrs. Huffington were the only ones there.

"Reporting for duty," I said with a salute as the door squeaked closed behind me.

"Come in, come in!" Mrs. Huffington gushed.

So I did.

"Paxton, Lisa, this is Evangeline," Mrs. Huffington said.

"Hey," we all said with a nod.

A few minutes later we were still the only ones in the classroom. "So where are the droves of students desperate for help?" I asked.

"Oh, they're on their way!" Mrs. Huffington assured me.

As if on cue, the door whooshed open, but it was Adrienne who whooshed in.

"Hey!" I said, jumping up.

"Yay! You signed up!" she said. "Hey, Paxton," she called with a wave, then slid a desk next to mine, keeping a watchful eye on the others as she whispered, "I looked all over for you at lunch today! Miss Ryder told me you were sitting by yourself on the sidewalk eating a cold burrito!"

"Only after I looked all over for *you*," I whispered back.

She rolled her eyes. "Mr. Vogel was a no-show at our choir practice, if you can believe that! But why weren't you in the quad?"

I shrugged. And not wanting to say too much in the presence of undeniably perked ears, I simply said, "I ran into Tatiana."

She gave me an empathetic "Oh."

"Actually, it went okay." I glanced over my shoulder, then whispered, "But I have so much to tell you!"

A handful of what appeared to be freshmen came through the door, so she stood and said, "Call me tonight, okay? Or come over. Can you come over?"

I nodded. "I'll call you when I get home."

She moved toward the door, saying, "You know what? Just come over for dinner."

I hesitated. Dinner at the Willows' with all the familial bantering was always so much fun.

"Six o'clock—be there!" Adrienne said, then waved goodbye to Paxton and pushed through the door, letting herself out and Roper Harding in.

I cringed. Roper Harding? Was this why they desperately needed chemistry tutors?

No wonder!

"Roper! Come in, come in!" Mrs. Huffington said. "You got my message?"

His oversized glasses seemed to lead his head in a bob up and down.

"Well, here she is!" she said, swooping a hand in my direction.

For the next forty-five minutes I tried to ignore oily zits, flecks of dust (or whatever that was clinging to his greasy hair), and insanely potent B.O. It was an exercise in extreme self-control, but the maddening thing was that Roper acted like *he* was the one tolerating *me*.

When it was over, he barely grumbled a thanks before jetting off to catch the late bus, leaving an almost visible stream of body odor behind him.

After he was gone, Paxton propped open the door, and Lisa said, "Mrs. Huffington, someone's really got to talk to him about his personal hygiene."

"I know," she said with a tisk.

"I'm not doing that again," I said flatly. "He's rude and he stinks."

"I know," Mrs. Huffington said again, with another tisk and a shake of the head.

It was obvious that Mrs. Huffington didn't know what to do about the situation. And as we filed out to her friendly "See you Thursday!" I muttered, "Not if Roper's back!"

Paxton, who was right behind me, chuckled and said, "Well, as of today, I don't have to deal with any of this anymore." He slipped the second strap of his backpack on. "I'm done!"

"You've completed twenty hours?" I asked, instantly jealous.

He grinned and nodded as we walked along. "And I'm not doing it again next year, that's for sure."

"Why didn't you do the Elf Extravaganza with the rest of the choir?" I asked.

He looked at me with a slight cock of the head. "I transferred here at semester?"

"Oh," I said in a big, stupid, stretchy-faced way. "Sorry."

He laughed. "Not a problem."

We were still walking along together. "So where'd you transfer from?"

"Missoula, Montana," he said, drawing out the vowels. I was reminded of the way I'd seen him sing during choir practice in the Performance Pavilion. Big O's, dropped-jaw A's.

He had a very expressive mouth.

"Tell me about Missoula, Montana," I said, mimicking the way he'd pronounced it.

We were approaching the parking lot now. "I don't know if we have time for that," he said. "Where'd you park?"

"Oh, I'm walking home."

He seemed surprised. Like walking was not something one did in Missoula, Montana. Or maybe not something one should do as a Larkmont High upperclassman. "You want a ride?" he asked.

I smiled at him. "Why not?"

We got into a sharp white Lexus (of all things), and by the time we reached the second intersection, I'd already heard a lot about Missoula, Montana. Not that I was absorbing it. I was too fascinated with the curls in his blond hair. With the curve of his sideburn as it swept back toward his earlobe. With the strong lines of his nose and cheekbones. With his lips. His lovely, expressive lips as they popped and pushed and projected words into space.

He reminded me of something . . . David of David and Goliath? A Greek warrior without the armor? He was different from other guys at school. He had a different *way* about him. He was more storybook . . . more *noble*.

Suddenly it struck me that maybe *that* was what I'd been doing wrong! Maybe I'd been looking for a fantasy kiss from ordinary guys! Bad boys, even. Maybe what I needed was a guy with an air of nobility! Some classic chivalry and charm!

By the time Paxton had pulled up to the condo, I was frenzied; consumed by the need to know! Did those noble lips hold a crimson kiss? Would they transport me to that world between worlds, where beating hearts and tender lips were all that existed? Where the dizzying spin of passion vanquished all else?

I had to know!

And so . . . I kissed him!

57

Cataclysmic Kissing

APPARENTLY PAXTON HAD NOT BEEN ADMIRING my expressive lips or anything else about me. Apparently he was just giving me a ride home.

My luscious lips were met with a single-handed push back and bugging eyes. "What was *that*?" he gasped.

"A kiss . . . ?"

"But I barely know you!"

According to my rapidly accumulating knowledge of the teenage male, this was not a standard complaint. But here he was, quite literally freaking out.

I was suddenly mortified. What had I been thinking? That I was so hot that any guy in the world would be happy to kiss me? This was sure one ice-cold bucket of reality!

"Why'd you do that?" he was asking.

I just shook my head and opened the door, desperate to escape.

"Do you have a *crush* on me?"

I looked back at him. "No!"

"Then why'd you kiss me?"

I got out of the car, frantically building a protective barrier around my badly bruised ego. This guy wasn't noble. He wasn't even *normal*. "Sorry if I offended you," I said. "It won't happen again."

And I was about to slam the door when he said, "I wouldn't tell Adrienne if I were you!"

I hesitated, *then* slammed the door. But as I let myself into the condo, I kept thinking, Adrienne? What's Adrienne got to do with this?

For someone who's supposed to be smart, I couldn't seem to wrap my head around this. In the back of my mind, there *was* a theory developing, but I didn't want to hear from the back of my mind. I wanted the back of my mind to leave me alone.

My father actually came in handy as a distraction. It wasn't just the memory of that morning's clash in the intersection, either. On the kitchen table I discovered that he'd left me a letter and a vase of hibiscus flowers.

"Who let him in?" I grumbled. "We moved here to get *away* from him." I turned on the kitchen faucet and shoved the flowers bloom-first down the garbage disposal. And as they were mincing up and getting gobbled down the drain, I ripped up his letter. His five-page mini book of justifications, rationalizations, explanations, and lies made lovely confetti. (At least I assumed that was what was in the five pages. I stopped reading after "Dearest Evangeline.")

The confetti, then, too, went down the garbage disposal.

I cranked up Velvet Revolver and ate a massive bowl of double-fudge ice cream through "Sucker Train Blues," "Do It for the Kids," and "Big Machine." During the next few tracks I faced off with a mountain of clothes that I'd tried on and tossed aside, skipping over "Fall to Pieces" when it started wailing. I shouted along during "Set Me Free" and "You Got No Right" and reveled in my favorite cut, "Slither."

Then, in the short interval before the next song started, I heard the telephone ringing, so I turned down the music and picked up the phone.

It was Adrienne. "Can you come over at five-thirty instead of six?" she asked. "Mom's got a class to go to at seven."

Thanks to my dad (and Velvet Revolver), I'd successfully forgotten what I'd been trying not to think about. But there it was again, louder than ever.

I desperately wanted to bail on going to the Willows', but the back of my mind was tired of being ignored. The back of my mind wanted to know if it was right.

"Sure," I said, like I hadn't a care in the world. "I'm on my way."

58

Vow of Silence

FAMILIAL BANTERING DID NOT PLAY A BIG ROLE at the Willows' dinner table that night. Mr. Willow (or Pops, as he's known to Brody, Adrienne, and me) was working late, and Brody had already left for karate class, so it was just us chickens.

"Hens," Adrienne corrected.

"Huh?"

"The *roosters* have flown the coop."

"Oh, right," I said, then added, "I can't believe Brody's still taking karate. He's been doing that since, what? Fifth grade?"

Adrienne nodded. "He tests for his black belt in two weeks."

"Wow." Mild-mannered Brody with a black belt. It seemed like an unexpected collision of opposite energies. "Wow," I said again.

Mrs. Willow beamed as she placed grilled salmon and veggies on the table. "We are so proud of him, aren't we, Adrienne?"

Adrienne nodded and changed the subject. "Are you ready for the world history exam?"

I groaned. The unit test was coming up on Friday, and I hadn't even organized my notes.

"I did summary notes if you want a copy."

"Yes!" I said. "You're a lifesaver!"

"I thought you two didn't have any classes together," Mrs. Willow said as she served herself some salmon.

"Oh, we have the same English and history teachers," Adrienne said, "just different periods."

"Well that's not so bad," Mrs. Willow said.

"Yes, it is!" Adrienne and I said together, then looked at each other and laughed.

So for a moment, for a brief, happy moment, I felt at home. I listened to Adrienne catch her mother up on school and choir and the whims of her geometry teacher, while I ate (with actual silverware) a healthy, balanced meal served on real plates. No paper, no plastic in sight; this meal was substance on substance.

Then Mrs. Willow deflated my mood by asking, "What about you, Evangeline? How is everything?"

I almost said, Fine, just because that's the easy, disposable answer. But this was Adrienne's mom. My mom-away-from-home mom. So I sighed and blurted, "It's a mess!"

"How so?"

Hmm. What did I want to tell her?

Not about school . . .

Not about kissing!

I chose the subject that would interest her the most anyway—my parents. "My dad's decided Janelle Phillips is not the one for him after all, so now he's trying to convince my mom to forgive him." I picked at my salmon. "I think she's falling for it."

She hesitated. "You mean they may be getting back together? Why, that's wonderful!" She turned to Adrienne. "Wouldn't that be wonderful?"

Adrienne gave her mother a look that said unmistakably, Back off!

Mrs. Willow took a deep breath, smoothed the napkin in her lap, and said, "Well, whatever happens, you're always welcome here."

"Have you got adoption papers handy?" I asked, trying to lighten the mood.

She chuckled, then said, "I don't think we'd be able to afford three in college. I'm worried about two! Besides, you'll be emancipated in, what, a year and another week or so?"

Oh, yeah.

My glorious birthday.

Whatever would I do to celebrate?

When dinner was over, Mrs. Willow wouldn't let us help with the dishes. "Shoo! You have exams to study for! Homework to complete!" She grinned over her shoulder as she made her way into the kitchen. "Boys to discuss!"

And that is exactly what Adrienne was dying to do. When we were alone in her room, she threw herself on her bed and said, "I want to hear everything that's going on with you, but first I've got to tell you . . . I think I'm in love!"

Uh-oh.

I managed, "Really?"

She sat up, bounced on the edge of her bed, and yanked me

beside her. "He's smart and cute and tall and *nice*. He's funny and complimentary and . . . and I think we've got chemistry! Lately when I'm with him, I feel all light-headed and electric! When he smiles at me, my insides turn to jelly!" She was really bouncing now, taking me along for the ride. "Can you guess who?"

Oh, no, I groaned on the inside. Oh, no-no-no.

My forehead was beading with sweat. My stomach was knotting. "Do I know him?" I asked as innocently as I could.

"Guess!" she squealed.

"I have no idea!" I lied.

"Here's a hint: He sings like an angel!"

I kicked into avoidance mode. "Well, does he like you back? Is this official? Are you saying you have a boyfriend?"

"No! *But*—lately he's been talking to me before choir, waiting for me after choir . . . and today he sort of put his arm around me as we went through the door." Quickly, she added, "It wasn't an official arm wrap . . . he was just being polite, letting me through the doorway first, but he didn't *have* to put his arm out; he didn't *have* to touch me!" She bounced harder. "Guess!"

"Let's see. He's in choir . . . he's tall . . ."

"Oh, come *on*, Evangeline! It's Paxton!"

The back of my mind said, Du-uh, while the rest of me withered.

"Paxton?" I asked, feigning surprise. "But you barely even acknowledged him in tutoring today!"

She looked enormously pleased with herself. "I played it so cool, didn't I?"

"I'll say."

"He is so different from other guys, Evangeline. He *thinks* about things. Music, books, politics . . . he's so interesting to talk to! He makes *me* think. I love that! I love the feeling that there's so much I haven't thought about before; that the world is full of so many . . . connections!"

She was glowing. And she sounded so . . . enlightened, whereas my mind felt like a panic-stricken blank.

All I could do was blink at her.

Blink, and vow to never, *ever* tell her what I'd done.

59

Give Me a Little Less Conversation

I DID TELL ADRIENNE A LITTLE about my kissing adventures with Stu and Andrew, but I avoided the subject of Eddie entirely and blocked Paxton from my mind. I kept the whole thing short and breezy, acting like it was all a big joke . . . which I was starting to think it might be.

Just not a very funny one.

When I got home, my mother tried to talk, but I wasn't in the mood for that, either. I knew where she was going with her seemingly innocent questions—straight to the subject of my dad.

I told her, "I do not want to talk about him," and managed to escape to my bedroom.

The door opened up a minute later.

I groaned, "Can we *please* just call it a night?" but she parked herself at the foot of my bed and said, "Not until I find out what you thought of his letter."

"I didn't *read* his letter."

"So"—she glanced around—"where is it?"

"With his flowers and my opinion of him—down the drain."

She took a deep breath and didn't say anything for a whole minute. Maybe two.

So I kicked out of my jeans (hers, actually), put on a nightshirt, and got into bed.

"Honey," she finally said, "you're not being fair to him, or to me."

"Not fair? Who's not being fair? First we move out of the house—I've got to adjust to all of that, *and* you bawling your eyes out for six months . . . now you want to do a U-turn and go right back?"

"What I want is for us to *talk* about things. Openly. With a counselor."

I snorted.

"Evangeline, look. *I'm* the one he wronged. And I'm deeply touched by your loyalty, but I need you to be on my side now, too. And if I'm going to be completely honest, I have to admit that there are things I should have done differently. It's not *all* his fault."

She was being so calm. So rational. And although something about what she was saying seemed off, I was too worked up to figure out what.

Besides, I had other things on my mind.

Bigger, more worrisome things.

Like my best friend being in love with a guy I'd recklessly kissed.

60

Risky Business

I WOULDN'T CALL WHAT I DID that night sleeping. And as if the conversations I'd had with Adrienne and my mother hadn't been enough to keep me up all night, the fact that my mom sneaked a call to my dad after she left my bedroom sealed the deal. I cracked my door open so I could hear, but apparently she noticed, because she closed hers tight. They had a long conversation, too. She finally put the phone back in the charger at two A.M., then poured herself three bowls of cereal.

Apparently reconciling with an adulterous jerk gives one a monstrous appetite.

When morning finally arrived, I was wiped out. And since I hadn't cleaned off my makeup before bed, my eyelashes were all caked and flaky, and there were dark smudges under my eyes. I should have started all over, but I was just too tired. I patched things up the best I could, downed some orange juice and an energy bar, and escaped the condo.

I knew Adrienne had choir practice before school, which meant that *Paxton* had choir practice before school, which meant, if I played it right, I'd have the opportunity to apologize to him, plead rash impulsiveness, and beg him not to tell Adrienne. After worrying about it all night, I decided that his comment about *me* not telling Adrienne was no guarantee that *he* might not let it slip.

Lady Luck, it appeared, had taken pity on me, because as I entered the side door of the Performance Pavilion, I saw Paxton—and he was alone!

"Paxton!" I called, hurrying toward him.

He froze when he saw me.

"Hey, it's okay," I said, but he obviously didn't think it was okay.

"Stop stalking me," he said between his teeth.

"I'm not stalking you! I'm—" And then I saw Adrienne approaching. She was up on the stage, only a few yards away. "Oh, there she is!" I said, smiling at her like I'd finally discovered her whereabouts.

"Hey!" she said cheerfully, then sat on the edge of the stage and gave Paxton a rosy-cheeked "Good morning!"

He smiled at her somewhat stiffly, then looked at me and walked away.

Adrienne grabbed on to me. "You didn't *tell* him, did you?"

"No!"

"Well, what were you saying to him?"

"I was just looking for you!"

Fortunately, she didn't ask *why* I was looking for her. And as soon as I could get away, I did. Obviously, apologizing to Paxton was risky business. Steering clear of him would probably be much wiser.

So with half an hour to kill before school, I found a quiet corner in the library and did the psychology worksheet that Mr. Stills had given for homework, longing the whole time for a frappuccino.

When the warning bell rang, I packed up and dragged myself across campus to math. We have six whole minutes from warning bell to final bell, and I still barely made it to math on time.

As I entered the room, I noticed that there was a flower on my desk.

A beautiful, pink hibiscus flower.

I approached as though it might attack me.

What was a hibiscus flower doing on my desk?

And there was a note, too!

A note that said *Evangeline* across the envelope.

My face flushed hot. How *dare* my dad harass me at school!

How *dare* he invade my . . . my educational space!

Weren't there laws about unregistered adults roaming campus?

Why hadn't someone stopped him and tossed him out on his ear?

What kind of place was this, where harassing fathers were allowed to roam freely through the halls, leaving emotional land mines on estranged daughters' desks?

I wanted to rip the petals into mincy little shreds. I wanted to crumple up the note and hurl it! But then I saw Robbie Marshall's face; his open, smiling, expectant face.

I collapsed into my seat as I realized that my father hadn't been there at all.

Robbie Marshall had.

61

"Edelweiss" at Ozzfest

THE NOTE SAID: *Will you go to the movies with me on Friday?*

I slipped it into my binder and deliberately did not look at Robbie for the entire class period.

It was my first real date invitation.

And it was from the hottest guy on campus.

It crossed my mind that maybe we'd just started out on the wrong foot.

Or, rather, the wrong kiss.

Maybe he was a redeemable kisser. Maybe he just needed some guidance.

What if he was willing to read *A Crimson Kiss*?

Hmm. Not likely.

And how embarrassing would that be? Here, Robbie—read this romance novel and then maybe we'll go out. He'd think I was a total dweeb. I'd *be* a total dweeb!

And aside from the kissing, what would we talk about? Sports? I couldn't hold up my end of that conversation. And he obviously didn't know much about blues-based rock. What did we have in common?

No, chocolates and flowers were nice, his *biceps* were nice, but I didn't really want to go out with Robbie Marshall.

I decided that the best response was simply to say I couldn't, no, *wouldn't* go out with him.

Unfortunately, this went over like "Edelweiss" at Ozzfest.

"Why *not*?" he asked, whininess tingeing his voice. "It's just a movie!"

I looked down at the flower, twirling it absently. "I'm sorry," I said lamely. Then I looked at him and asked, "Why'd you pick this flower?" I realized that the question wasn't clear, so I added, "I mean a hibiscus flower. Why not a daisy, or a, I don't know, *snap*dragon."

He laughed. "There's such a thing as a snapdragon?"

I couldn't help smiling back. "Yeah. Would have been a more appropriate choice, huh?"

He took the flower from me and put it in my hair so the stem rested on my ear. "This is a vacation flower. A have-fun flower. A gone-surfing flower." He was standing very close to me now and was smiling. "The movie starts at seven-thirty. Can I pick you up at six? Take you out for dinner?"

Slowly, I shook my head. "I'm sorry, Robbie. I already told you no."

He grinned. "But the flower's saying yes!"

It was cute. Very charming. And I almost, *almost,* caved and said why not? But it just didn't feel right. "I really appreciate everything, Robbie, but . . . I just can't." I took the flower off my ear, put it on his. "You go have fun without me," I said quietly.

Then I turned and walked away.

62

Accounting

When I met up with Adrienne at break, the look on her face jolted me right back to the fiasco with Paxton. "What's the matter?" I asked, praying that she was upset about something, anything, besides me kissing the new love of her life.

"There are rumors," she said, holding my arm and pulling us both into a sitting position on the edge of our cold, very hard brick planter in the quad. "Rumors about you."

"Such as . . . ?" I asked, still praying that Paxton wasn't involved in these rumors.

"Rumors that you've gone mad kissing people. I knew about Robbie and Justin and Blake, of course, and last night you told me about Stu and Andrew, but people are saying you've also kissed Eddie Pasco and Trevor Dansa! It's just gossip, right? You haven't actually kissed those guys, right?"

The name Paxton had not left her lips.

My whole being felt washed with relief.

"Why are you smiling?" she asked. She gave a little squint. "I know that smile . . . that's a guilty smile! So you *have* kissed them? When? Why didn't you tell me?" Her squint grew severe. "And Trevor *Dansa*? What were you thinking?"

I gave a little shrug. "It was a diversionary tactic to stop Eddie from talking about a dream he'd had that involved me and honey."

"You and *honey*?"

"Exactly. Trevor was there, so I grabbed him and kissed him."

She put a hand in front of her mouth and shook her head. "You are out of control!"

"No, I'm not."

She leaned in a little. "Kissing some random guy to avoid another guy you've kissed is definitely out of control! You are never going to find the perfect kiss that way!" Then she mocked me, saying, "A crimson kiss does not reside on the lips of Trevor Dansa—even I know that!"

She had me there. But I pursed my lips and held my ground. "That was a mistake, okay? But I am in control. I am *so* in control." I put my fists on my hips. "You want to know how in control I am? I turned Robbie down for a date this morning."

The warning bell rang.

"*What?* Oh my God. How am I supposed to keep up with you?" She stood up. "And why didn't you tell me about Eddie last night?"

I looked down. "You were excited about Paxton, and everything you said made him sound so . . . terrific." I shrugged. "Which made the whole thing with Eddie seem ridiculous." I smiled at her. "How are things with Paxton, anyway?"

"Weird," she grumbled, then hurried off to class.

63

Barking Up Trees

I *WAS GREATLY RELIEVED* that my kiss with Paxton hadn't been part of the gossip Adrienne had heard, but I couldn't help feeling a little queasy that people were talking about Eddie and Trevor. And even though I had my (very rational) explanations, it *did* seem a little out of control.

Things did not improve at lunchtime. I hadn't packed myself a lunch, so once again I was stuck in the Snack Shack line. Only this time instead of being accosted by Sunshine Holden, this girl named Jan Pratkay cut in line and stood uncomfortably close to me. "Your problem," she said conspiratorially, "is that you're barking up the wrong tree."

I delivered an extremely sharp-witted "Huh?" but a moment later her meaning crystallized in my brain.

Jan Pratkay, you see, is a lesbian.

I'd met Jan in middle school, but since she was never really a friend, I chalked up her ninth-grade transformation from quiet girl with long, auburn locks to spiky-haired tough chick as teenage rebellion.

"Coming out" was not part of my vocabulary at the time.

But when someone finally clarified things for me, I figured, Oh. Well, that makes sense.

And while I halfway expected another confrontation from Sunshine over the hibiscus-flower incident, I never in a million years saw *this* coming.

I took a step back from Jan and said, "By 'barking up the wrong tree,' you're referring to the whole forest as opposed to, say, a *particular* tree?"

"Assuming the forest is full of boy trees, that's right."

This was one bizarre conversation.

I took a deep breath. "Well, the forest I'm barking in is just fine with me."

She laughed. "You are so in denial."

"No . . . ," I said, keeping my voice low, "I'm not."

"Don't deny it until you try it . . . ," she said, grinning.

"Uh, Jan?" I asked, easing away from her. "I've heard that you just know. Like, from a very early point in your life, you just know. Isn't that right?"

One shoulder bobbed with a shrug. "If you listen to yourself."

I caught up with the rest of the line. "Well, I've listened, and I know that the forest I'm in is the right one for me."

"Look," she said with a pragmatic air. "Rumor is you've gone crazy kissing guys. I'm just saying that what you're looking for may not be in the place you're looking for it."

"Look," I said back, "it's a big forest! There are a lot of trees! I just haven't found the right one yet."

She finally gave up and returned, presumably, to her own shady glen, but she'd left me with a pounding headache. I dragged myself to the quad to meet Adrienne and tell her about these strange new developments, but Adrienne wasn't there. And rather than chase all over campus again trying to track her down, I just parked on the ground and unwrapped the turkey sandwich I'd bought in an effort to eat something better than a sucky burrito.

What I discovered was that the bread was soggy, the lettuce was slimy, and the mayonnaise had . . . *eeew* . . . little black specks. Maybe these specks were pepper, but with the way my day had gone, I couldn't help imagining they were bits of bug legs.

I wound up chucking it in the trash.

64

Hitchin' a Ride

AFTER SCHOOL I FOUND BRODY'S TRUCK idling in the parking lot. "Hey, Bro," I said, leaning in the open passenger window. "Can I hitch a ride?"

"Sure," he said.

So I got in, and to my surprise he put the truck in gear and released the brake.

I looked out the window. "What about Adrienne?"

"She had something going on after school."

It was somewhat strange being in the truck alone with Brody. The pattern we'd fallen into was that if Adrienne was staying after school, I walked. But here we were, alone in the truck, him being a conscientious, polite, and law-abiding driver, me feeling exhausted, famished, and uncomfortable with the weird silence between us.

I turned on the radio, which was already tuned to my favorite station. "Steady as She Goes" by the Raconteurs was playing.

"Looking forward to graduation?" I asked in a lame attempt to get a conversation going.

"No," he said as he eased into the exit line.

"No? How can you not be looking forward to getting away from this insanity?"

"I actually like it here," he said, then added, "And Connecticut's not exactly next door."

I sat up and turned down the radio. "Wait. You were accepted at Yale? Already?"

He nodded, looking straight ahead.

"Congratulations!"

"Thank you." He glanced at me. "I wish I was as enthused about it as you."

"Are you kidding? I would die to go to Yale!"

He glanced my way again. "You think you might?"

A cloud gathered quickly over my exuberance. "I don't know if they'd accept me." I sighed. "And what's tuition?"

"As you would say, insane. But you're smart and resourceful. . . . I'm sure you could get a scholarship."

"Did you get one?"

He nodded. "I wouldn't be going if I hadn't."

We talked about college and majors, and he advised me to apply to schools early, and when we got to the condo, I smiled at him and said, "Congratulations again, Brody. That's awesome."

He nodded. "Thanks."

I thought he was going to say something more, but he didn't. So I got out of the truck and waved. "See ya!"

He waited for me to get inside the condo okay, then put his truck in gear and purred down the street.

65

Clam Chowder

THERE WERE NO FLOWERS or notes or other appetite-killing surprises waiting for me at home, so I was free to gorge myself on whatever I could find to eat.

Raiding the refrigerator didn't yield much. I ended up making a Velveeta sandwich, which doesn't qualify as real food, but I was desperate.

Then, re-inspired by Brody's acceptance into Yale, I settled in at my desk and got serious about my homework. Finding the equations of rotated conic sections in math was pretty straightforward, and I took extra care in the graphing, using a blue pencil for the ellipse and a red one for the rotation.

I admired my handiwork when I was done.

Nice!

I did the usual tedious Wednesday-night word search handout for Spanish (ridiculous waste of time, if you ask anyone in that class) and the assigned reading for Miss Ryder. And I actually buckled down and studied for Mr. Anderson's world history test. The copy of Adrienne's notes was a godsend!

So I was feeling extremely happy with myself, and flirting with the idea of walking the five blocks to Taco Bell for something more enticing than a Velveeta sandwich, when my mother unexpectedly jangled through the door.

"Hey!" I called, forgetting that I was upset with her.

"Surprise!" she said, depositing her purse and keys and an overflowing sack of groceries on the kitchen table.

I pawed through the sack. "Oh, thank you!" She'd brought a bag of salad, French bread, clam chowder, croutons, milk, orange juice, deli cold cuts, a gorgeous tomato, and apples. "I am starving!"

She smiled. "So let's eat."

She did try to broach the subject of my dad during dinner, but I pointed at her with my spoon and said, "Not while I'm eating," which actually made her laugh and say, "Okay."

So she talked about work—personnel gossip mostly, but she had some pretty entertaining customer anecdotes, too, and a hilarious story about sticky, icky apple juice all over Aisle 5. And midway through my scrumptious bowl of chowder, it struck me how happy she seemed.

How much she was laughing.

How her eyes were twinkling.

How her smile was back.

There was, of course, only one explanation.

My dad.

I watched her and wondered how a man who had caused her so much pain could still make her so happy.

66

Mysterious Phone Call

BEFORE BED I cleaned off two days of makeup, snipped some split ends off my hair, took a piping hot shower, listened to my favorite cuts from *Surrealistic Pillow* (which did, unbelievably, include "White Rabbit"), and vowed to make a fresh start in the morning. I was going to pack a nutritious lunch! Ace every quiz that got thrown at me!

I was also going to forget about the bad kisses and find a good one.

Brody had called me smart and resourceful, and it was time I applied that to kissing. I needed to figure out what made a kiss crimson! I needed to find a better way to make my fantasy a reality!

I sat up in bed reading segments of *Welcome to a Better Life*. It helped me feel like I was in charge—like my actions would have positive reactions and happiness could be mine if I just believed I deserved it.

And I did deserve it!

I did!

In the morning, I packed a lunch, coordinated a sizzling outfit of my mom's jeans, a sparkly tank top, and a fur-trimmed hoodie, applied some fresh makeup (including some shimmering eyebrow highlights), slipped in oversized hoops, and headed for school.

This was a new day!

A new beginning!

I felt good!

My new beginning started with Robbie Marshall ignoring me during math. I should have been relieved, but I wasn't. He'd been really sweet the last few days. (And he was, undeniably, hot.) Did I just miss the attention? Or maybe there was a rumor circulating about me being a lesbian and he was mortified to have kissed a gay girl.

The thought suddenly gripped me.

What if people thought I was gay?

Aw, what's it matter? I told myself. If the dweebs at this school want to think so, what do you care?

At break Pico Warwick, class joker and chum-to-all, came up to me and swept me up onto the quad stage, where he made an exaggerated show of dipping me backward and planting his smackers directly on mine. It was so ridiculous, so Hollywood, and so Pico that I couldn't do anything but laugh when I was upright again. People clapped and whistled while he made a grand bow and I curtseyed, and for the rest of the day I felt great.

And when stinky, oily Roper Harding came in for tutoring and Mrs. Huffington *insisted* that I help him, I stood up and walked out. I'd find some other way of doing community service. Something real. I'd feed the homeless! Paint City Hall! Pick up trash at Prager Park!

Anything was better than twenty hours of smelling Roper Harding.

When I got home, I was jonesing for something sweet to eat, so I went directly to the freezer.

The double-fudge ice cream was gone (a casualty, no doubt, of late-night conversations my mom had had with my dad). There were vestiges of vanilla-orange swirl in a half-crushed carton, but it was more ice crystals than ice cream, so I set it to melt in the sink.

Besides, I didn't want vanilla-orange swirl. I wanted chocolate! Deep, rich, bitter chocolate. There had to be some somewhere!

The phone rang as I was ransacking a cupboard.

"Unless you've got chocolate, go away!" I shouted into cans of beans and boxes of couscous.

The person on the other end ignored my command.

Or perhaps they had chocolate!

On the sixth ring I scrambled to answer the call. "Hello?" I panted.

A voice whispered, "You're nothing but a stupid tease."

Before I could fully absorb what I'd just heard, the line went dead. It had been a girl's voice . . . but whose?

Sunshine's?

It had been disguised as a baby-girl voice, so it was impossible to know.

I laid the phone carefully on the counter and stared at it for a full ten minutes. And as much as I told myself that the call had been mean and stupid, I still felt icky inside.

The condo number was unlisted—who besides Adrienne would have it?

When I thought enough time had passed, I pressed star-sixty-nine.

After twenty nerve-racking rings, a man answered the phone. "Hello?"

It was a voice I didn't recognize. "Hi. I missed a call from a friend? I'm not sure whose house this is?"

He laughed. "It's not exactly a house. It's a pay phone outside of Starbucks."

"The one in the Baldwin Center?"

"Yeah," he said.

I thanked him and got off the phone, racking my brain.

Adrienne would never do such a thing.

Who else had my number?

67

The Halls of Hell

CLUES TO THIS LITTLE MYSTERY began surfacing the following day. I was still reeling from Mr. Anderson's insane history test when Adrienne came rushing up to me at break and blurted, "Someone's writing your name and phone number on urinals."

"On *urinals*?"

"Brody told me. It's in the boys' bathroom in the four hundred wing and in the five hundred wing. It says 'Call me! Kiss me!' then your name and phone number. He's already talked to the janitor—they're going to clean it off."

I gasped as I connected the dots. "I got a crank call from someone last night."

She gasped, too. "No!"

"But . . . it was a girl."

Her eyes were enormous. "What did they say?"

So I told her the whole story, and she said, "Well, if they were disguising their voice, maybe it was a guy!"

"I *thought* it was a girl, but now . . . I don't know!"

"Don't worry," she said, putting an arm around my shoulders. "We'll figure it out."

My heart swelled. Even though my going after a crimson kiss was something she didn't entirely get, Adrienne had really tried to help me. And now, despite the fact that she thought my kissing had gotten out of control, was she abandoning me?

No!

Adrienne Willow was more than just a friend. She was my ally! Someone who would get to the bottom of who'd done this! Someone who'd make sure that the creep who'd turned me into target practice didn't get away with it!

I hugged her and said, "Tell Brody thanks, okay?"

The bell rang. "Why don't *you* tell him?" she called, hurrying off to class.

So despite everything, I was actually feeling okay until some guy with bushy sideburns (who I'd seen around campus but didn't actually *know*) came up from behind me and said, "You Evangeline?"

"Huh?"

He eyed me up and down with a disgusting grin. "Ooooh, baby!" he laughed, and hurried off.

All through third period I felt flushed and angry.

So I'd kissed a few guys. So what!

Then between third and fourth I heard exaggerated kissing sounds. I looked around for the source, but it could have been any of a number of people. And during fourth I could feel people staring at me. I wanted to stand up and shout. "Get a life, people! I didn't *do* anything!"

I was so relieved to see Adrienne at lunch. She joined me in the quad, whispering, "It's bad out there."

"I know! I can't *believe* this."

She unearthed her lunch. "I ran into Brody after third. I told him you were very grateful."

"I *am*," I said. "I don't know what I'd do without the two of you!"

I unwrapped my homemade sandwich and Adrienne's eyes popped. "Wow, where'd you get that?"

"I'm trying to eat better."

She nodded. "Well, that's a good start!"

But after a few minutes Adrienne said, "You know, maybe we should start eating lunch somewhere else."

I looked over my shoulder to the place she was watching.

It was the "popular girls," packed in a little huddle, trying not to look like they were doing what they were obviously doing: talking about us.

Or, more likely, me.

"Maybe so," I said.

But just then a high-volume howl cut through the lunchtime chatter and someone came crashing out of the 100-wing's boys' bathroom.

The quad fell quiet.

Everyone turned to look as Travis Ung limped away from the bathroom.

Then suddenly Blaine York came thudding through the door, followed by some dreadful thumping and crashing sounds. Then Justin Rodriguez staggered out, blood streaming from his nose.

"Oh, no!" Adrienne cried, dumping her sandwich as she shot to her feet. "Brody!"

"Brody?" I asked, following her to the scene. "Where?"

He emerged from the bathroom, calm and collected, with not so much as a scrape on him.

"Wait," I said to Adrienne. "*Brody* beat them up?"

Adrienne gave me a look that danced between pride and despair. "Oh, this is bad. This is very, very bad!"

The quad began to buzz with collective disbelief as people crowded in to see the winded, staggering carnage that was Justin, Blaine, and Travis. Everyone was asking the same thing: "Brody Willow downed three guys?"

Unfortunately for Brody's spotless behavioral record, it was true.

68

Call Me Stupid

CALL ME STUPID, but I didn't fully grasp my role in what had happened until I saw the Magic Marker rolling across the walkway.

Going after Justin Rodriguez . . . writing my number on his hand in the biology room . . . it all felt like a lifetime ago.

Adrienne tried to intervene as three teachers escorted Brody and the battered boys to the office, but the teachers already had their hands full and Brody shooed her off.

"He's going to get suspended!" Adrienne wailed when she was back with me. "And they'll never advance him to black belt!"

"I can't believe he beat them up," I said, my jaw still dangling over the whole scene. "Why didn't he just turn them in?"

She stared at me, pinched her eyes closed, flared her nostrils, opened her eyes, then shook her head. "I've got to go," she said flatly, then turned and left.

"Hey, wait!" I called, but she was gone.

After lunch, chemistry was just a blur. All I could think about was Brody decking Justin. I'd always thought of Brody as my somewhat nerdy older brother, but the nerdy part was now gone. He'd wiped out three decent-sized guys at once! Nothing nerdy about that.

And my heart swelled again because, more than ever, I felt like part of their family. My own family was a mess, but Adrienne and especially Brody had come to my defense in ways I'd never imagined.

As Mr. Kiraly's middle fingers poked the chalkboard and flipped birdies through the air, I wondered how Brody's meeting with Hickory Stick Hershey was going. Somehow I doubted he'd get off with writing letters of apology. Graffiti, obscene language, insubordination, cheating, stealing, smoking . . . these were all things you could get away with at Larkmont High.

Brawling was not.

I began to feel claustrophobic. The classroom felt like a box—a sweltering box where I was trapped with thirty other glazed-eyed people desperate to escape.

Particles of chalk dust danced in the air. Why did this room still have chalkboards? Why not whiteboards? Why were we having to breathe in chalk dust instead of toxic marker fumes?

The chalk dust began to feel like a blanket that I couldn't breathe through. I was suffocating. Smothered. And Mr. Kiraly's voice . . . it was a Hungarian torture device, booming chemical conversions in my ear, echoing . . . echoing . . .

When the bell rang, I escaped the classroom in record time. I began running, dashing past people, dodging them, squeezing between them. There was only one class left in the school day, but I couldn't bear the thought of being locked up for another fifty minutes.

I needed to find Brody.

Find out what had happened.

Thank him.

Somehow that seemed so much more important than going to psychology.

My plan was to walk to the Willows' house. I was sure Brody had been suspended, and that that's where he'd be. What I wasn't sure about was how to leave campus without permission. Having never given it serious thought before, I had no idea how much stealth was involved in ditching school.

What I discovered was it's easy. To ditch school, you simply *leave*. No one asked where I was going, no one asked for a hall pass. . . . I just walked away.

No wonder Larkmont has such a truancy problem!

I left the way I always leave: through the student parking lot. To my surprise, Brody's truck was still there . . . and Brody was in it, reading his physics book.

I guess you can suspend a guy from school but you cannot make him leave.

"Hey, Chevy-man!" I said, opening the passenger door.

He seemed surprised. "Evangeline?" Then he looked at his watch. "You're going to be late to psychology!"

It flashed through my mind that him knowing I had psychology sixth period was odd. But Brody's a fact magnet, so I just chuckled and said, "You're suspended and I'm ditching . . . who'd have thought?"

He chuckled, too. "Not me."

"I was actually on my way over to your house to thank you."

He blushed.

"Really, Brody. You didn't have to go and get yourself suspended." I grinned at him. "You should have just let *me* beat them up." Then I added, quite seriously, "I feel bad that you're in trouble over me. And Adrienne says you won't be eligible for your black belt now, which I know is a big deal. Is that because you're only supposed to use karate in self-defense?"

He shrugged and nodded. "I'll have to go before a review board. It'll just take longer."

"So how long are you suspended from school?"

"A week."

"A week! How long did Justin and his cronies get?"

"They've got detention."

"That's it?"

He nodded.

There was a moment of awkward silence, and then I blurted, "Well, I don't know what to say. I'm sorry this got you in trouble." I shook my head. "It's been a really sucky year, but I'm glad I've got you and Adrienne looking out for me. You're like the brother I never had, Adrienne's like the sister I never had.... Your parents are even like the parents I *wish* I had."

He was looking at me in a peculiar way. Confused? Embarrassed? Uncomfortable? I wasn't sure. With Brody, you don't really talk about feelings. You talk about science. Or math. Or how to maximize compound interest. I was treading on new territory here, and it was obviously making him uneasy.

So I laughed and gave him a sisterly hug (something I've done a lot of over the years), then said, "Look, Brody, I'm just trying to say thank you, all right?"

But as I pulled away, I found myself face to face with him.

Looking him in the eyes.

And before I knew what was happening, we were kissing.

69

Attempting to Re-establish Sanity

IT WAS THE SWEETEST, dearest brotherly kiss.

And weird.

How could I have just kissed Brody?

Or wait. How could *he* have just kissed *me*?

As I pulled away, I felt confused and embarrassed and incredibly awkward. "Wow. Uh . . . *well* . . ."

Being a man of many words, Brody just blushed.

I sat there a moment, then opened the passenger door and started babbling. "Well. I'm going to walk home now. I'm going to walk home and clear my head and . . . and cut my hair. Yeah. I think I'll go cut my hair."

"Don't cut your hair again," he said. "I like your hair!"

"Well," I said, my hands flitting around my head, "I'll probably just snip it a little here and there."

How mature of me. We'd just shared a semi-incestuous kiss, and I was now discussing hair-cutting strategies.

"I gotta go," I said, and took off.

He didn't follow me in his truck, didn't run after me, didn't even honk the horn in an effort to get me to come back and talk.

It was probably the smartest thing he could have done, because I didn't *want* to discuss it. I wanted to forget it.

Unfortunately, two monster bowls of the fudgeaholic ice cream that I discovered in the freezer did nothing to help.

So I cranked up *Ride the Lightning* by Metallica, and from "Fight Fire with Fire" through "Creeping Death" I let it bash my worries away.

It wasn't until the opening strains of "The Call of Ktulu" that I realized someone was bashing on my door.

"Evangeline! Evangeline, it's Adrienne! Open up!"

Before I could fully consider the potential repercussions, I turned off the music and whisked open the door.

Adrienne rushed in and handed me a book. "I couldn't find the movie. I know he has it somewhere, but I couldn't find it. All I could find was the book. It's his favorite book."

"Who? What are you talking about?"

"Brody! You have to read this, okay?" She pressed the book on me. "You have to read this, and then you will understand that he is in love with you."

"What?" I looked at the worn milk-chocolate-colored cover with gold lettering. *"The Princess Bride?"* I gave her one of her own trademark squints. "And he can't be in love with me! He's practically my *brother.*"

"Yeah, well, he's already got a sister, and I don't think he's looking for another one." She held her forehead. "Don't you get it? All those times we tried to set him up . . . all those times we kidded him about letting us find him a hot girlfriend . . . he's been in love with you!"

I collapsed into a living room chair. "This is not good."

"You're telling me!" She sat in the chair next to me. "I got an inkling of it the other day when he said, 'As you wish,' but I couldn't quite believe it. After today I *totally* believe it!"

"What was that 'As you wish' about, anyway?"

She pointed frantically to the book. "You have to read that!" She leaned way over toward me and said, "Evangeline, he is the sweetest guy! What are we going to do?"

My face contorted into what must've been a horrendous sight.

"What?" she asked.

"I kissed him," I blurted. "Or he kissed me. I don't know. We kissed."

She jumped out of her chair. *"What?"* She looked at me like I'd just murdered someone. "When?"

I grimaced. "Today. During sixth period. In his truck."

"How *could* you?"

"I didn't plan for it to happen, I didn't *mean* for it to happen, I'm not even sure *how* it happened, it just did!"

Her head quivered side to side. "I can't believe you! How could you have kissed Brody when you don't even *like* him!"

"I had no idea he liked me!"

"So what! You don't like *him*. It's not fair to kiss people you don't like!"

"But—"

"You are totally out of control! Who *won't* you kiss?"

"What?"

She threw her hands in the air and said, "I've got to get out of here. This is so unbelievable."

"Adrienne, wait!"

But for the second time that day she hurried off, only this time she slammed the door.

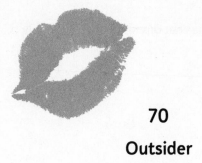

70

Outsider

I WAS AFRAID TO CALL ADRIENNE over the weekend; afraid to go over and try to talk to her; afraid (for the first time in my life) to run into Brody.

So I stay holed up in my room, reading *The Princess Bride*.

It served as excellent parent repellent. Every time my mother looked in, I was obviously doing something studious; and the unwritten rule is one does not disturb one's child when they're studying. (Never mind that I was reading about a dreaded pirate, a sweet farm boy, a beautiful maiden, a disgusting prince, and a Spanish swordsman who lived to avenge his father's death.)

It was a fantastic book. Funny, moving, inspiring... and yet Sunday afternoon when I'd finished it, what I felt was heartache.

"As you wish" really meant "I love you."

What was I going to do? I loved Brody, but I wasn't *in* love with him. He was nice-looking—it wasn't that. He was smart and kind and obviously heroic (in a karate chopping sort of way). But to me he was *family*.

What was I going to do?

Fortunately, I had the condo to myself because my mother was off doing "sneaky shopping" for my birthday. And fortunately, there was still some fudgeaholic ice cream in the freezer to help me think.

There was no sense in using a bowl.

These were desperate times!

I went directly at it with a spoon.

And while I ate, I ruminated.

I deliberated.

I contemplated.

And with the carton finally scraped clean, I concluded that there was really only one thing to do:

I needed to talk to Brody.

I considered calling. The phone, with its appealing remoteness and its emergency abort feature (otherwise known as the end button), seemed like the safest way to go.

But it was also cowardly.

So I took a shower (two days of reading in bed will make you feel matted all over), flossed my teeth (I don't know why—they just wanted flossing), and left the condo. No makeup, no agonizing over clothes, no earrings—I just pulled on some jeans, a T-shirt, and sneakers, and I left.

On the walk over to the Willows' I tried out every opening line I could think of. I didn't know how in the world to say what I wanted to say.

Actually, I didn't know *what* I wanted to say. "I'm so sorry!" seemed like a good start, but what exactly was I sorry for? Until the kissing incident in the truck, I'd never been anything more than chummy with Brody. It's not like I'd been leading him on! And who'd kissed whom?

How could I not know?

So I was already completely muddled when I walked past my old house and saw my mother's car.

Once again it was parked beside my father's.

I stood there for a moment staring. So much for "sneaky shopping."

I hurried on, but when I neared the Willows', I saw Brody and Adrienne sitting side by side on the steps of their porch. They were deep in conversation, and even though they were probably talking about me, I couldn't seem to find the courage to join them.

I eased back and watched from the shadows of the neighbor's tree. The bow of their heads, Adrienne's comforting rub of Brody's back . . . it was all so quiet and gentle and warm.

I felt like a ghost by that tree. A ghost of the girl I used to be, stuck somewhere between worlds.

Between families.

71

Swinging

I ESCAPED MY OLD NEIGHBORHOOD . . . the Willows, my parents, the hibiscus plants in glorious bloom. . . . I hunkered down, kept my eyes on the ground, and just walked away.

I didn't go through the graveyard to be with other ghosts. I went a few blocks beyond it, to my old elementary school. I don't really know why. It's just where my feet took me.

The place was deserted, as schools should be on Sundays. It was also totally accessible, as schools should *not* be.

I wandered past the kindergarten classrooms, their windows plastered with artwork. I thought about Mrs. Potts, who had been my kindergarten teacher, and wondered if she was still alive. She'd seemed so old, with her graying hair, long skirts, and tatty moccasins. Every day she'd wear those same moccasins. The little beads had fascinated me. How did they hold on day after day? When would the frayed strings finally give up? How would we ever find all the beads as they bounced and scattered across the black-and-white squares of the linoleum floor?

My life now felt like Mrs. Potts's moccasins. The strings had broken. The beads had scattered.

How would I ever put it back together?

I sighed and moved on, passing by my first-grade classroom, home of Mrs. T (short for Tottenicker). She had been one of those teachers who rarely smiled, and only with great effort.

I had not been a fan of Mrs. T.

I walked around the corner to Room B-8, which had been my second-third combination with Miss Escar. She'd been so hyper, and loved to hug all her students good morning. I'd adored her, living for my morning hug and trying to steal extras throughout the day.

I peeked in the B-8 window. The same familiar *You're a STAR* pencil mug was on the desk. How many years had it been?

Nine?

I suddenly ached for a hug from Miss Escar.

Then there was my old fourth-grade classroom with its presentation platform, where Mr. Dixon had gotten us comfortable with speaking in front of the class. Every week we had to "present," and after a while it was no big deal.

It was also the platform my dad had used when he'd come as a special guest. He'd played guitar and talked about music, and everyone thought he was the coolest dad ever.

For me, that had been a *huge* deal.

I continued meandering through campus, peeking inside the windows of all my old classrooms, feeling a little like Alice at ten feet tall. Eventually I wound up at the playground and sat on the low curb that held in the sand surrounding all the play equipment.

I ran my fingers across the sand, through the miraculous grains of disintegrated rock. I thought back to how I'd accidentally skip-loaded heaps of it home in my shoes; how my shoes and the dunes they contained had been banned to the porch, leaving scattered piles of the fine tan grains outside.

Sand was a big part of life then.

And now?

When was the last time I'd thought about sand?

I got up and trudged over to the swings, where Adrienne and I used to try to loop over the top. Way, way high we'd swing, catching air, thumping hard as gravity reclaimed us, trying again, thumping again, twisting and crashing and squealing.

I sat on one of the hard rubber seats and pushed off. The seat felt snug against my hips, the chain warm in my hands. I leaned back and held my legs out. I pumped and pulled and drove myself higher. Higher. Higher. I pumped until I thought the swing might break, until the chain might pull apart from the frame. Then I scooped through the air a few more times, coasting back and forth, panting, my stomach becoming queasy, the earth starting to spin.

I ground to a halt and staggered away, my insides completely topsy-turvy.

72

Ditch Day

"WHERE HAVE YOU BEEN?" my mother demanded when I finally dragged myself home around eight o'clock.

"Swinging," I answered glumly.

"Swinging?"

She was looking at me skeptically, so I unlaced a shoe and shook sand into the trash.

"But why?" she asked.

I shrugged. "Felt like it, I guess."

She studied me a minute, then stroked my shoulder and said, "Honey? Is there something you want to talk about?"

I shrugged again. "I'm fine. I'm just tired. I think I'll take a shower and go to bed."

She didn't pry, which I really appreciated. But in the morning I still felt . . . quiet. I looked through the clothes I'd slowly been collecting from my mother's boxes and realized that I didn't want to wear any of them.

I wanted my own jeans. My own tops. My own *face*.

When I left the house, I had every intention of going to school. But then I took a detour to Starbucks for a wake-up frappuccino, which led to me taking a seat in a comfy corner chair, which led to me ditching school.

I just didn't have the energy to face anything about school.

Not the incomplete homework.

Not Robbie or Justin or Andrew or Eddie or Stu or Paxton or Trevor.

And especially not Adrienne.

I just didn't know what to say to Adrienne.

Besides, if Brody was suspended for saving me from urinal ill repute, shouldn't I be suspended, too? It didn't seem fair that he was kicked out for something I'd put into motion.

I thought about going over to the Willows' to talk to Brody, but bottom line, I chickened out. Instead, I whiled away the morning sipping a grande mocha frappuccino and rereading *A Crimson Kiss*.

The disturbing thing was, I couldn't get into it. I tried to escape into its pages, tried to get swept away by the story, but it just felt so . . . flat. And the harder I tried, the more empty I felt. Betrayed, almost. Like when I needed it most, it just didn't deliver. The words were just words. They no longer *spoke* to me.

I knew I couldn't blame the book.

It was me.

What was *wrong* with me?

73

Escape

I FINALLY LEFT STARBUCKS and started walking to the only place I could think to go.

"Bubbles?" Izzy said as I pushed through the Groove Records door. He was obviously not completely awake, as it was only eleven (still early by musician standards) and the store had just opened.

"I'm ditching," I grumbled. "And you'd better not rat me out."

He chuckled, "Me? You gotta be kidding." He leaned his forearms on the counter and said, "But what's got you so bent?"

I put up a hand. "Izzy, please. I'm in crisis mode. I'm here to escape. Can you just put on some music?"

"Crisis mode? Hey . . ." He came from around the counter. "What's going on, Evangeline?"

I raised my eyebrows. Evangeline? He'd never called me *Evangeline*.

He'd also never looked this serious.

No, *concerned.*

I looked at him and suddenly realized that Izzy wasn't just my dad's old mentor. He wasn't just the guy who ran Groove Records. He was somebody who'd been in my life ... forever.

He was actually my friend.

It flashed through my mind that it would be easy to do the ol' my-parents-are-making-me-miserable routine, but I didn't want to. Except for Adrienne, I hadn't really talked to anyone about school, and now I was even having problems with her. And although there was no way I was going to tell Izzy about my kamikaze kissing, I suddenly did want to tell him *something.* So I shrugged and said, "Things have been kinda rough at school lately."

He looked at me thoughtfully. "How so?"

"I don't know." I started shuffling through a bargain bin of pre-owned CDs, just to avoid looking at him. "I just feel kind of *lost.* Like my friends don't really know who I am anymore." I laughed, but there wasn't much humor in it. "Actually, it's more like *I* don't know who I am anymore." I looked at him. "I feel like I don't know what I'm doing, or even what I want."

He nodded, and for some reason he seemed so wise. So centered and sure and steady. "Well, what do you *care* about? That's where you've got to start. What do you really *care* about?"

What did I care about? I paused and gave it some thought. A crimson kiss? That used to be what I wanted, but now I wasn't so sure. Especially after this morning, when the book had just left me flat. Maybe it was more the passion of it. Maybe that's what I wanted more than the kiss.

The passion.

To really, really care.

He saw my hesitation. "May I make a suggestion?"

I shrugged.

"Sometime the things we really want are right there in front of us. We just don't see them." It was his turn to shuffle through the CDs. "I've actually been thinking about you and your dad since the last time you were here."

"Aw, Izzy, *please*."

I turned to go, but he stopped me. "No, no! I'm not talkin' about your family problems. I'm talkin' about the music your old man's turned you on to. Stevie Ray, Eric Clapton, Jimi Hendrix—"

"Robert Johnson, Muddy Waters, Chuck Berry, yeah, yeah, he's definitely covered rock and the blues," I said, feeling completely exasperated. Izzy obviously had no idea what I was going through—why had I even opened my mouth?

But then he said something that completely threw me. "What about the chicks?" he asked. "The, uh, *women* of rock?"

I blinked at him.

"You didn't know about Grace Slick. That really shocked me. What about Janis Joplin? Aretha Franklin? How about Bonnie Raitt?"

This seemed so out of left field. I didn't know *why* we were having this conversation. "I've heard of them, of course."

"But didn't your old man ever *play* them for you?"

I shrugged. "I've heard cuts on the radio...."

"But you haven't *studied* them like you have the guys." He was suddenly very . . . agitated. He was starting to twitch all over. His shoulder, his neck, his *other* shoulder . . . "So to you the blues, hell, *rock*, it's a man's world."

Before I could fully process this statement, he leaned in and said, "Evangeline, you've been coming here since you were knee high to a grasshopper. You know more about music than most musicians. You *care* about it more than most musicians. I keep expecting you to take up guitar, but you haven't. You never even stick your nose inside the guitar room. Why not?"

I just stared.

I didn't know why not.

He pulled me along through the store, saying, "You want to escape? You want to know who you are? *This* is how you do it."

74

Rock School

Izzy PULLED a worn blond wood guitar off the wall. "Fender Strat—classic Clapton guitar." He plugged it into a large, tattered black amplifier. "Marshall amp—classic Hendrix, Clapton, hell, anybody amp."

He strapped the guitar over my head and helped me get comfortable. It was heavier than I'd expected.

He flicked down some switches on the amp, and a short while later it was letting off a buzz, which for some reason made my heart start pounding.

Just touching the strings made a sound.

A cool, powerful sound.

"Forget scales, forget theory, forget songs," Izzy was saying as he positioned my fingers on two strings. "Say hello to the power chord."

"Hello, power chord?" I joked, afraid to move.

He laughed and handed over a guitar pick. "Play!"

"Play?"

"Play!"

So I took the pick and I hit the strings.

It sounded thuddy.

He repositioned my fingers a little and said, "Try again."

I hit again, and this time the strings rang.

He twisted the knobs on the amplifier. "Again!"

So I hit again, and suddenly the room, my arms, my whole *body* was filled with an awesome sense of power.

"Again!" he said when he saw my wide eyes.

So I struck again.

And again!

"Wow!"

"That's my girl! *That,*" he said, moving in, "is an E power chord." He repositioned my fingers. "*This* is an A . . ."

Switching between E and A was a thrill. A rush. A . . .

"Isn't that a *gas*?" Izzy asked.

"Yes!" I laughed.

He introduced me to a few more chords, showed me a basic riff, then left me alone to practice. And did I practice! When I finally left Izzy's, my fingers were aching and blistered, and I was in the best mood of my life.

I knew how to do the riff to AC/DC's "Highway to Hell"!

(It was pretty crude, but still!)

Brody and kissing and school (which had already been out for over an hour) were the farthest things from my mind. I cruised home, singing, "I'm on the highway to hell! On the highway to hell!"

Which, unfortunately, is exactly where I wound up.

75

Roadblocked

As it turns out, my mother had also ditched. Seeing her in the kitchen startled me, but I tried to act nonchalant as I said, "Oh, hi."

"Oh, hi," she said evenly, then immediately called my dad. "She's here." She kept the conversation brief, then looked at me and said, "I got an automated call from the school this morning, informing me that you were absent."

They did that? They had no system for stopping mass murderers or drug dealers from traipsing around campus, but they had automated attendance security?

What kind of insane priorities did our school have?

"Oh, God," I said with an exasperated sigh as I hurled down my book bag. "Does everything always have to be such a downer?"

She ignored my question and instead crossed her arms and said, "Adrienne also called, looking for you. She thought you might be sick."

I rolled my eyes and plopped into a chair.

"I asked her what was going on with you, and I finally got it out of her."

"Oh?" I gave a little squint. "So tell me—what *is* going on with me?"

"Apparently you've become a serial kisser."

"A *what*?"

"Those are her words, not mine."

"She called me a serial kisser?" I flipped my hands up and rolled my eyes. "That's the most ridiculous thing I've ever heard! So I've kissed a few guys, so what?"

"Well, apparently your name is winding up on urinals, and boys are getting suspended on your behalf, and people are confused by your kisses."

"Oh, *God*. Why couldn't she just keep her mouth shut?"

"Because she cares about you, that's why!"

"She's *mad* at me, that's why! She's trying to get *back* at me, that's why!"

My mother took a deep breath and said, "Tell me where you've been all day. Have you been out kissing people?"

I laughed because it was such a bizarre question. And really, would I say yes if I had been? "I was at Groove Records," I said. "Didn't kiss a soul."

"You were at Izzy's? All *day*?" She said it like she both didn't believe it and was afraid it might be true.

"All day," I said. "Izzy taught me how to play guitar."

She blinked at me, her mouth suddenly pinched into a little knot.

"See?" I said, sticking out my swollen and very pink fingertips.

The doorbell rang.

"Oh, *great*," I grumbled. "I can't believe you called Dad. There's no way I'm talking to him." I sat up a little as she headed for the door. "I'm actually extra mad at him—why didn't *he* ever teach me how to play guitar?"

But it wasn't my dad. It was Adrienne. In tears. Flushed and hyperventilating. "You," she said, pointing a shaky finger at me, "are no longer my friend! I want nothing more to do with you or your psycho lips! You stay away from *me*, you stay away from my *brother*, and you stay away from Paxton!"

"Paxton?" my mother asked. "Who's Paxton?"

"The guy I'm in love with!" She turned to me and screamed, "You knew I was crazy about him and you *kissed* him!"

"I *didn't* know!" I cried. "Adrienne! I—"

She left, slamming the door, so I charged after her.

Unfortunately, I found myself roadblocked by my dad.

76

The Clash

It took ten minutes of struggling and screaming and trying to get out the door before I finally gave up. Adrienne was long gone, and something about my parents fighting together against *me* completely wore me out.

And while I was panting in a chair, trying to recover, my mother told my dad everything Adrienne had told her.

"A serial kisser?" he said, looking at me in disbelief. "Good God."

I glowered at him. "Quite the puritanical reaction from someone who's cheated on his wife."

"Stop that, Evangeline!" my mother commanded. "His behavior doesn't justify yours! His behavior doesn't have anything to *do* with yours!"

The room fell deadly quiet, which my dad fixed by saying, "Does it? Is this your way of acting out against your mother and me for getting back together? Because if it is, it's not going to change anything. Your mother and I are working things out, and—"

"And that's something most kids would be thrilled about," my mom said, her eyes pleading. "Honey, most kids whose parents split up *want* them to get back together; to be a family again. If I can forgive him, that should be the end of it!"

The whole earth seemed to spin for a moment as I finally figured out what was wrong with her logic. I blinked at them both, then slowly rose to my feet. "This is *not* about just the two of you! It quit being about the two of you when you had *me*. It's about the three of us." I turned to my dad and said, "It's about the trust *I* had in you. About the faith *I* had in you. About the belief *I* had that I was your 'angel' and that you would always be there for me!" My chin was quivering and my eyes were brimming. "You told me, you *promised* me, that you would be and I believed you. Idiot that I was, I believed you!"

I bolted into my room and wedged my chair up against the knob. Then I threw myself onto my bed and sobbed my heart out.

77

Puffy Eyes

THE NEXT MORNING I woke up wiped out, with horribly puffy eyes. "Oh, great," I moaned into the bathroom mirror, then staggered into the kitchen to retrieve the herbal compress.

My mother and father were at the kitchen table, drinking coffee.

"Oh, great," I moaned again, yanking open the refrigerator.

"Ready to talk?" my mom asked calmly, her coffee mug poised at chin level.

I grabbed the compress and staggered back to my room. "I'm not going to school," I said flatly.

"Then we're not going to work," my mother said. "We'll be right here when you decide you'd like to try to talk this out."

I staggered back to my room and fell asleep for about an hour, but when I peeked out my bedroom door, they were still there.

Once again I felt trapped. And I considered escaping through the window, but where would I go? My eyes made me a one-woman freak show. Once upon a time I would have run straight to the Willows', but that fairy tale had come to an abrupt (and unexpectedly tragic) end.

So I stayed put. And I didn't actually spend much time brooding about my parents. What was the use? They were going to do what they wanted to do.

Adrienne was the one I couldn't stop thinking about. I had to find some way to explain things to her. I hadn't set out to kiss her true love first. I wasn't a backstabber with psycho lips! I was her best friend!

But in the pit of my stomach I didn't feel like a best friend.

And as I sat trapped in my room, it occurred to me that all this heartache might be for something that didn't even exist. What if there was no such thing as a perfect kiss? What if it was some unattainable ideal that only existed in movies and between the covers of a book?

But *Adrienne* was real. Her friendship had been real. She'd been there for me through everything! I couldn't imagine my life without her.

No, I had to find some way to explain.

I had to apologize.

I had to fix things!

But she was at school, and I wasn't about to go there with my insanely puffy eyes. So I sat down at my desk and wrote her a note. A letter, actually. I explained everything and told her how sorry I was, and how much I appreciated what a great friend she'd been and how I'd do anything to get her to forgive me.

After reading it over, I realized that it was disjointed and rambling, and that I'd forgotten to say a few things.

I'd just begun rewriting it when my father came into my room. "What do you say we all take a walk?"

I looked over at him. "What do you say you walk yourself right out of my room?"

My mother was next. "Please, honey, you need to come out here and talk."

"No, I don't," I told her.

Around eleven-thirty my father tried again, this time bringing with him a sandwich flanked with apple slices.

I gave him a searing look. "What makes you think you can just come in here?"

He sat down anyway and tried to talk, but I ignored him and his pathetic peace offering. Finally he went away.

I rewrote Adrienne's letter four times. I kept adding things, changing things. And when I'd completed the fourth rewrite, I discovered that I'd absentmindedly eaten most of the sandwich and apple slices. "Moron," I grumbled. And because I was obsessing to the point where I had eaten the enemy's food, I declared the letter to be good enough. I folded it, origami-style, into the shape of an envelope, wrote Adrienne's name on the outside, and put it in my pocket. Then very quietly I wedged my desk chair up against my doorknob, and for the first time in my life I escaped my parents through a window.

78

Jagged Halves

IT MADE NO SENSE to go to the Willows' house and wait. School was in session for another two hours, and afterward Adrienne would (most likely) have stories to cover or songs to sing. So despite my bedraggled state, I walked to school and waited for Adrienne outside her fifth-period class. I made no eye contact with anyone. I just stood by, my heart beating faster and faster as the end of class neared.

When Adrienne appeared, she threw her nose in the air and marched past me. "Here," I said, falling in step beside her. "Please read this."

She refused to take the letter.

So I forced it on her, and her response was to rip it in half.

"Nothing you can say will make this better," she said, and threw the halves at me.

I watched in disbelief as she walked off. We'd been friends, *sisters* our whole lives. How could she not even read what I had to say? I'd spent the entire day agonizing over it, and in one measly second it was in jagged halves at my feet.

I picked up the pieces, licked my wounds a moment, then left school.

79

Revelation

I MIGHT HAVE LEFT THE LETTER on Brody's windshield, but Brody was suspended, so there was no windshield. And I might have gone to the Willows' to apologize to Brody and explain everything (as best I could, considering I didn't really understand it myself) and ask him to talk to Adrienne, but I wasn't that brave.

So instead I went to the Willows' and left the two halves of my letter on their welcome mat. I splayed them slightly, the jagged edges touching at the bottom and separated at the top. To me it looked like a broken heart. To anyone else it probably looked like a pathetic, ripped-up note.

When I returned to the condo, my father's Mustang was no longer parked out front.

Hallelujah.

My mother, however, was still parked inside.

And she was fuming.

"We've been worried sick about you! We finally broke into your room and discovered you'd snuck out the *window*. Where have you been? What have you been doing?"

"Look. I've got bigger problems than you and the jerk!"

"Stop that!" she snapped. "He's your father! Why are you so unforgiving?"

"When I can forget," I snarled at her, "*that's* when I'll forgive."

"It works the other way around!" she shouted as I locked myself back in my room.

Around seven o'clock I snuck into the kitchen, got the phone, and called the Willows'. "Adrienne," I said when she answered. "Please don't hang up."

She hung up.

I tried again.

She didn't even answer, and midway through the recording of their message machine, it clicked off. Like somebody had yanked it out of the wall.

I tried again.

The line beeped endlessly with a busy signal.

I skulked back to my room and just lay on my bed looking up at the tacky cottage-cheese-textured ceiling. I thought about Adrienne and wondered how in the world I was going to make things right. Why wouldn't she at least listen? Didn't we have enough shared past to get us through this?

Then somewhere in the back of my mind, I heard a sound. A distant, whooshing sound. Like someone whispering through the cracks around a bolted steel door.

"Hyp-o-crite," the voice whispered. "Hyp-o-crite!"

Slowly, eerily, my skin began to crawl.

I sat up, wrestling madly to close the door, but the voice blasted it open.

"Hyp-o-crite!"

And there it was—a mind-blowing revelation.

I'd been acting just like my dad.

And Adrienne was acting just like me.

80

Ice Cream Therapy

STANDING FACE TO FACE with my own hypocrisy was hard. And it was easy to rationalize. What I'd done didn't *compare* to what my dad had done. Impulsively kissing a guy was nothing like breaking your marriage vows! Anyone who thought they were comparable was insane!

Still, the cold winds of my conscience wouldn't let me close the door. And in the end I had to face the heart of the issue: How could I expect Adrienne to forgive me if I wasn't willing to even *try* to forgive my dad?

I had no idea how to answer that.

And so I ate ice cream.

My mom joined me at the kitchen table but said nothing. She simply scooped her own bowl of double fudge and sat down across from me.

After my dish was empty, I pushed it away and went straight for the carton.

My mother hates when I eat out of the carton, but she didn't raise an eyebrow, didn't say a word.

As I scraped the bottom, I finally broke the silence. "How did you stop being angry?"

Her spoon tinkled against her bowl. "I guess I just became willing to let it go." She looked at me directly for the first time since she'd sat down. "Anger is a fuel that can only carry you so far." She shrugged. "I guess I started looking for an alternate energy."

"But how *do* you do that?"

She thought a minute. "It started with your father wanting to talk things out. Seeing what the other person is feeling is hard when you're feeling so much yourself, but that's what you've got to try to do. In our case, what happened had nothing to *do* with you." She reached across the table and took my hand. "But your dad and I were so wrapped up in our own feelings that we didn't see what we'd *done* to you." She squeezed my hand. "Evangeline, I'm so, *so* sorry."

And in that moment of weakness I blurted, "Mom, I had this *awful* epiphany tonight," and told her everything I'd been going through to try to talk to Adrienne.

Midway through my story, a knowing smile crept across my mother's face, and when I was done, she shook her head sympathetically and said, "Just like your father."

I nodded. "Exactly."

"So where does that leave us?" she asked.

I looked into the empty carton and sighed. "Needing more ice cream."

81

Resident Shrink

My mom didn't try to force the issue with my dad. Instead, she helped me see that I needed to do something about the mess I'd made for myself at school. "I had some time to think about this while you were locked in your room, sweetheart, and I think it wasn't just the book that made you go after all those kisses. I think it was a way of acting out against your dad."

"It was not!" I said.

"Maybe he made you hate men?"

"I don't hate men! And I'm not a lesbian!"

She looked shocked. "Who ever said anything about you being a lesbian?" Then very quickly she added, "Not that there would be anything *wrong* with that."

I rolled my eyes. "Look. I just wanted to change my life. To take *charge* of my life. And you know what? It helped a lot. You and Dad dragged me down so bad. You were mopey all the time, he made it so I couldn't go out for volleyball—"

"You could have, and you *should* have."

"Oh, right." I shook my head and took a deep breath. "Anyway, I was only trying to *live* a little."

"Okay . . . ," she said after some consideration. "But the real question is, what are you going to do about the mess all this 'living' has gotten you in?"

"I don't know," I grumbled.

"Well, there's Adrienne, and there's school. You do not want to be the kind of girl who gets her name scrawled on urinals."

"I know."

"So? Any ideas on how to undo the damage?"

I scowled at her. "Obviously you have some."

She cocked her head a little, as if she was very clever and about to give me the golden key to solving my problems. "I've heard that in situations like this, it helps to apologize to the people you've hurt." She took a deep breath. "Maybe you should start by apologizing to everyone you've kissed."

"*What?* That's insane! Nobody apologizes for *kissing*. Kissing's like holding hands used to be when you were in high school. It's . . . it's like saying hi!" I leaned forward. "Besides, what would I say? 'I'm sorry I kissed you'? Like that wouldn't be more insulting than totally ignoring someone for the rest of his life?"

She eyed me. "Kissing is not like holding hands. And it's certainly not like saying hi."

I leaned back and shook my head. "You're living in a distant era, Mom."

She gave me a little smile. "Refresh my memory, would you? Why is Adrienne so upset with you?"

I stared at her, unable to come up with an even remotely logical retort. And long after our conversation was over, the things she'd said lingered.

But apologize to everyone I'd kissed?

That was insane!

How dweeby did I want to be?

Weren't things bad enough?

82

In Search of Lips

So yes, it was insane, but I set out the next morning to find them, all of them, and apologize. (Well, except for our class joker, Pico Warwick, and the Starbucks guy.) I didn't know exactly what I was going to say, and thinking about it petrified me. So I just made a list of names on a three-by-five card, checked it twice, marched to school, and began scouring the campus.

No lipstick victims in the quad area.

None in line for breakfast at the Snack Shack.

None between the 200 and 300 wings.

Or between the 300 and 400 wings.

Or between the 400 and 500 wings.

Where were all the lips?

Here I was, poised with apologies (of admittedly questionable content), and no one to deliver them to!

I moved over to the south part of campus and started checking there. And I was rounding the corner of the 900 wing when I spotted my note-passing classmate from psychology.

"Andrew!" I called (in an embarrassingly exuberant way). "Andrew, wait up!"

He turned and looked at me like he wasn't quite awake, but he quickly realized that a frenzied girl was charging toward him.

"Andrew!" I said, panting as I skidded to a stop. "I . . . I just . . ."

He now looked wide-eyed. Alarmed.

"Don't worry! I'm not going to kiss you!" I took a deep breath and said, "I just want to apologize for that incident outside of psych class. I was kind of a jerk and I know it and . . . and I'm sorry."

Gee. Such eloquence.

Which also didn't seem to be working.

He was still looking at me in a very odd way.

"Andrew?"

He blinked. "Yeah. Okay. Thanks."

But it didn't *feel* okay.

It felt like he was actually hurt.

"Look," I said, "I've had an emotional train wreck of a year, and I was . . . I don't know what I was doing. I'm just sorry, okay? I didn't mean to hurt anybody's feelings, certainly not yours."

"It's cool," he said, then gave me a sweet smile. "Maybe someday we can even the score?"

I laughed and said, "Oh, you don't want to kiss me. I'm a confused mess!" I stepped away from him, saying, "But thank you, Andrew. Thanks for understanding."

Already I felt lighter. Happier. I checked Andrew's name off my list and hurried toward the quad in search of another pair of lips.

Almost immediately, I spotted Stu, who was hanging out with Sunshine.

As if Sunshine's presence wasn't enough to make me go AWOL on Stu's apology, I started wondering why he was even on my list. *Stu* was the one who'd approached me that day at lunch. *He'd* been the one who'd kissed *me*. I didn't owe him anything! I might, arguably, even be mad at *him*. After all, he'd wanted a *rating*.

What did he take me for?

A kiss-o-meter?

But with a cringe I realized that even if I didn't owe Stu an apology, there *was* someone in the quad I probably did owe one to.

I just wasn't sure I was brave enough to deliver it.

83

Continued Quest for Ill-Begotten Lips

SUNSHINE HOLDEN WAS VERY SUSPICIOUS. "What do you mean you're sorry? I thought you hadn't done anything wrong!" Then she started mimicking me in a bitter, singsongy way. "It's not what you think, Sunshine. I have no intention of coming between you guys, Sunshine. He's all yours, Sunshine."

"Look," I said, trying to focus on my purpose (which did not include getting into a catfight), "I didn't mean to cause any problems, or hurt anybody in any way."

"Well, guess what? You did."

I nodded once and said, "I understand that now, and I'm sorry."

Somehow this emboldened her. She took a step toward me, saying, "Like that makes it any better?"

There was only so much groveling I was going to do. She wasn't even on the original list! So I put up both hands and said, "I'll leave you two alone now," and took off.

Between the 100 and 200 wings I pulled out my three-by-five card and crossed off Stu Dillard's name.

Two down, six to go.

But as I continued my before-school quest for ill-begotten lips, Stu suddenly came up from behind me. "Is this part of a twelve-step program?" he asked with a playful smirk on his face.

"Stay away," I warned, looking behind him for Sunshine.

Instead, he moved toward me, asking, "How's that work? First you admit you have a problem, then you apologize to everyone you've hurt, then you go through the other ten steps . . . ?" His smirk grew bigger as I backed away. "I notice you didn't apologize to me."

"Stay back!" I said. "I didn't kiss you! You kissed me!"

"I know," he said, smiling broadly.

"And I don't have a problem, I was just . . . confused!" Then I added, "And it obviously didn't hurt you in any way!"

He was still smiling. "Why don't you let me straighten out some of that confusion?"

I squared off with him. "This is not a game, Stu. And I don't care what you think, it's not a sport! So just go back to Sunshine and leave me alone!"

"Ooooh," he said as I pushed past him. "You are *sexy* when you're mad."

"On a scale of one to ten?" I tossed over my shoulder. "That line doesn't even rate."

84

Crossing a Threshold

As I escaped Stu, I couldn't help thinking about what he'd said about my being in a twelve-step program.

How insane was that?

I wasn't addicted to kissing!

I hadn't kissed anyone in ... *days.*

But (despite Sunshine's reaction) the apologizing *was* making me feel better. So when the warning bell rang, I went directly to math and waited outside the classroom for Robbie Marshall.

He looked at me warily as he approached.

"Hey," I said, suddenly tongue-tied. We hadn't really spoken since the hibiscus flower incident.

He could have just ignored me and walked by, but he stopped. "Hey," he said back.

Then we just stood there.

The hustling throngs of students on their way to class began thinning out.

Still, we just stood there.

"I'm sorry," I finally blurted. "I just want to say I'm sorry." And when it came out, I realized that I really, truly, was sorry. "You were so nice with the chocolates and the flower and looking up Stevie Ray. . . . I'm sorry about everything."

He, also, looked hurt. "Why'd you come on to me if you didn't want me?"

"I was an idiot, okay? I was confused." That sounded like a complete cop-out, so I heaved a big sigh and said, "I've been a basket case all year. My parents were getting divorced, I had to move, I . . . I started obsessing over this book about the perfect kiss . . . I don't know. I'm kind of a mess."

He pursed his lips slightly and nodded. "My mom and dad split up three years ago. It was the pits." He snorted, then gave a little shrug. "It's why I started lifting."

It was like seeing a single snapshot of the past three years of his life—his transformation from smart boy to dumb jock suddenly made complete sense. And I was so grateful that he understood that tears stung my eyes. "Healthier than kissing," I joked, blinking the tears back.

He smiled. "Hey, it's okay. I'm not *mad* at you or anything. Actually, it's made me think about some things."

"Oh, yeah?"

Our student sixth sense told us that the bell was about to ring, and as we headed into the classroom, he said, "I'd really like to get to know you, Evangeline."

I stopped and blinked at him.

He laughed at my reaction. "And you know what? I could use some tutoring in this class. I am so lost."

I smiled at him as the bell rang. "*That* I can do."

♥ 246 ♥

85

Behind the Bleachers

I DON'T USUALLY RUN INTO JUSTIN RODRIGUEZ. He hangs out in different parts of campus than I do. (Like in Mr. Webber's stinky biology room with his buddies Blaine and Travis, or the boys' bathrooms with his pet Magic Marker.)

This was probably a good thing, because when I was making my apology list, I'd put Justin at the bottom.

In pencil.

Inside parentheses.

Did I really need to apologize to someone who'd written my name on urinals?

But at break he unexpectedly appeared in front of me, flanked by Travis and Blaine.

It was like an omen: *There he is, just do it.*

They did a bumbling U-turn when they saw me, but I caught up to them and said, "Justin, wait up."

Justin did not want to wait up.

Justin wanted to escape.

I circled around him and planted myself. "I'm sorry I asked you to meet me at the gazebo. It was a mistake, I shouldn't have done it, and I'm sorry."

He stared at me, not moving a muscle. His cheek had a nasty bruise, and his lower lip was swollen and split near the corner.

Luscious lips they were not.

Finally he said, "Is this a joke?"

I shook my head. "It's an apology."

He pulled a face. "I don't get you."

"Look, I started it. Brody ended it. The stuff in the middle? That was all you." He didn't offer up an apology of his own, so I shrugged and moved on.

Four down, four to go.

Concentrating in Spanish and American lit was (for once) not a problem. I'd sniff down the others at lunch. (Or, in Brody's case, after school.) Then I'd be ready to move on to the grand finale:

Adrienne.

Apologizing to Trevor Dansa was easy because Trevor Dansa didn't care. "You already explained," he said. "Eddie was hassling you."

Oh, right, I thought. And knowing Trevor and his academic tunnel vision, he probably had no clue about bathroom brawls or serial kissing.

Thank you, Trevor Dansa!

"Okay," I said as he put the one earbud he'd removed to listen to me back up to his ear. "Just making sure."

Eddie Pasco, on the other hand, was *not* easy. For starters, I couldn't find him. I scoured the Snack Shack line, the quad, the alcoves surrounding the boys' locker room, the football field . . . I must've walked two miles looking for that boy!

Not finding him was, I confess, something of a relief. My brain could dismiss him as a smooth-talking stoner, but every time I saw him, my lips had remnant tingles from our kiss in the gym.

Eddie Pasco had undeniable magnetism.

Bottom line—he was dangerous!

But then, with a lightning bolt of deductive reasoning, I knew where I'd find him.

Behind the football field bleachers.

Never in my life had I gone behind the west-side bleachers. Besides being the place where stoners were known to party, it was also not a place you just happened to stumble upon.

You only went there with the intention of going there.

You have to walk clear around the track (or cut across the football field) to reach the bleachers. And to get to the notorious eight-foot strip behind them, you have to go down a narrow corridor between the concession stand and the bleachers.

For stoners it's perfect. It's a place to go in broad daylight and toke on weed or light up bongs or whatever stoners do to get stoned. They're hidden, but between the slats of bleachers they can easily see anyone who's coming to bust them.

Knowing this, I felt very self-conscious as I crossed the football field.

Were people watching?

Did they think I was hiking over to join them?

That I wanted to be a serial-kissing *stoner*?

And was Eddie even there?

Was he crowing to his friends about how irresistible he was? *I knew she'd come back for more, man, I just knew it.*

I felt small in the openness of the playing field. What was I doing? Why didn't I just wait until after psychology class let out?

But my feet were in motion, and they marched on. "Eddie!" I shouted when I reached the bleachers. "Eddie, are you there? I want to talk to you!"

There was no acknowledgment. Just the feeling that darkness was studying me between the slats.

"Eddie!" I called. "Come out here."

His dreamy voice drifted like smoke through the seats. "Why not come back here?"

I crossed my arms. "Look, if you're not coming out, I'll just say this from here." I liked that idea better, actually. No face-to-face with his dangerous magnetism. Just voice-to-voice with a stoner.

But a few moments later he sauntered out from the shadows, his soccer ball in hand. "Hey, hot stuff," he said with a comfortable grin, "here to dance?"

I dug in mentally and said, "Actually, I know you're going to think this is totally stupid and lame and all of that, but I'm here to apologize."

An eyebrow arched slightly as he moved toward me, tossing his soccer ball lazily from one hand to the other. "For what? Being a hot chick?"

He was close to me now, but to my great relief his magnetic pull was not working. Maybe it was blocked by my realization that there was something truly pathetic about spending a beautiful spring day hiding behind bleachers getting high.

"No," I said. "I'm apologizing for coming on to you at the dance."

He hesitated, then his brow furrowed. "You're kidding, right?"

I shook my head. "I know it's dorky, but that's why I'm here. I just wanted to say I'm sorry and clean the slate."

He was now looking suspicious. "You in a program?" he asked.

I laughed. "You're the second person to ask me that. No!" Then I looked him in his bloodshot eyes and ran the risk of totally overstepping. "But I've heard they work."

"Huh?"

I nodded at his soccer ball. "That should be your future, Eddie." I cocked my head at the bleachers. "Not that." I shrugged. "You know they don't go together."

Then I turned around and cut back across the football field, not caring at all that in Eddie Pasco's book, I'd probably just gone from hot chick to complete dweeb.

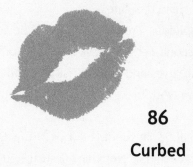

86

Curbed

EDDIE DIDN'T EVEN SHOW UP for sixth period. There was nothing I could do about that, but I *could* still try to smooth things over with Paxton. So when the dismissal bell rang at the end of school, I went directly to the student parking lot. If there was no after-school choir practice, odds were Paxton would be heading for his car like the rest of the drivers. If there was choir practice, I'd just wait in the parking lot until it was over.

I found Paxton's white Lexus, no problem. (Larkmont isn't one of those schools where Mercedes and BMW and Lexus models glint like so many diamonds in the parking lot sun. We've got a couple of acres of B-list brands, and the few "cool" cars are mostly restored and lowered.)

The bumper-to-bumper exit lines formed fast. Speakers started thumping; horns honked as cars jockeyed for position and peeled out of the parking lot and onto Larkmont Boulevard, leaving bluish puffs of smoke behind.

It took a good fifteen minutes, but then it was quiet except for the occasional mom cruising in near the Performance Pavilion side of the lot to pick up her kid.

Clearly Paxton was staying after school, so I parked myself among construction trucks on a comfy yellow SCHOOL VEHICLE ONLY cement curb two aisles over from the Lexus and waited.

I didn't mind waiting. I wanted to be done with this; wanted to get it behind me.

Unfortunately, I'd been so intent on checking another name off my list that I hadn't thought about how *Adrienne* might be getting home.

Brody's truck had not been in the parking lot.

Of course not.

He was suspended.

But sitting on the curb, I realized suddenly that it *would* appear. It would appear at the appointed hour to pick up Adrienne after choir practice, because that's the way Brody was. Quiet, punctual, reliable, considerate.

My stomach tied into a knot just thinking about him.

And then I heard laughter. Tinkling, joyful, familiar laughter. I turned, and there was Adrienne, walking beside Paxton. She was glowing, hanging on his every word.

They weren't holding hands, they weren't even walking that close together. But he was laughing, too, enjoying being the center of her attention.

I stayed stock-still on the parking curb as they approached the Lexus. I didn't want to interfere; didn't want to ruin this moment for her. In all the years I'd known her, I'd never seen Adrienne look this way. Even when she'd been around Noah in middle school, she'd never looked like this.

Paxton chirped open the door locks of his car, then held the passenger side open for her.

Spotting me was not an issue—they only had eyes for each other.

Adrienne ducked in as gracefully as a girl with an oversized backpack can, then beamed up at him as he closed the door for her.

Moments later he was in the car and driving off.

I watched them go, feeling a strange mix of love and loss.

87

Shut Out

On my walk home I took inventory. I had no friends, my hard-won GPA was probably history, living a fantasy had become a fiasco, and I was turning seventeen the next day.

Talk about having the blues. What kind of mess had I made of my life?

My fingers were still very tender, but I had the sudden urge to play some power chords. The afternoon I'd spent playing guitar at Izzy's was one of the only really great days I'd had all year. Maybe it would get my mind off things.

Maybe I could master that AC/DC riff.

Or maybe I'd just make mood-bashing *noise*.

But when Izzy saw me inside his store, he hurried over and said, "Oh, hey. I'm really sorry, but I've got to close up for a little while."

I had my heart set on playing, so I asked, "Can I hang out in the guitar room while you're gone?" I smiled at him. "You know, lock the door and let me shake the walls?"

Izzy had left me alone before while he'd run out to do an errand, so I didn't feel at all weird asking. But he was looking over his shoulder now, avoiding eye contact with me, acting very uncomfortable. "Uh . . . actually, I probably won't be coming back today."

It felt like he didn't *trust* me, but I told myself that I was being paranoid. And since the lights were still on and music was playing through the speakers, I said, "Can I just go play a few chords while you close up? I'll leave the minute you're ready to go."

"Sorry," he said, escorting me out. "Maybe tomorrow." Then he closed the door in my face, flipped over the OPEN sign, and flicked off the lights.

I left there feeling shut down and totally bummed out. I had no one. No*where*. And as I walked away, what shot through my heart was clear and simple:

I wanted my mother!

88

Salting the Soup

I RAN ALL THE WAY to Murphy's Market.

"Sweetheart?" my mother said when I faced her across the checkout scanner.

My eyes pleaded as I whispered, "Can you take a break?"

Without a word to me, she pushed a button on her PA announcement microphone and paged a checker to her lane. Within five minutes, we were out of the market and walking through the sunshine toward the Soup Savant, three doors down.

"What happened at school?" she asked.

So I told her about my apologies, I told her about Robbie and his parents' divorce, I told her about seeing Paxton and Adrienne together and how much I needed Adrienne to forgive me. And when I was done with that, I just broke down and blurted, "I feel like I've lost everything! I feel like I belong nowhere!"

I didn't want her to tell me everything would be fine—it

would have been a Band-Aid on what felt like a gaping hole in my heart.

My chin quivered helplessly as I talked.

I salted my soup with tears.

And my mom sat there, even-keeled and strong.

And listened.

89

Considering a Dismount

My mom offered to talk to Adrienne and I almost took her up on it, but in the end I decided that it was something I needed to do myself.

When I got home, my heart practically leaped through the door ahead of me.

The phone was ringing!

Maybe it was Adrienne!

She'd read my note! She'd forgiven me! And she was, of course, dying to tell me about Paxton!

I punched the talk button. "Hello?"

"Evangeline?"

"Yes?" I gasped, realizing who it was and wanting desperately to hang up.

"It's Brody."

"Hi," I choked out.

"I read your note," he said. "The one you left on our porch?"

I nodded.

He didn't say anything more, and it finally occurred to me that he couldn't hear me nodding. "Oh," I managed.

"I know it was to Adrienne, but . . . it helped."

"Oh," I said again, my mind a maddening blank.

"I'm sorry things are weird." His voice was choppy. Like he couldn't get any air.

"Me too," I said, feeling terrible.

"Is there anything I can do about it?" he asked.

There was something so sweet, so incredibly kind about that question. A massive lump formed in my throat as I choked out, "Forgive me?"

He hesitated. "There's nothing to forgive. And if you want to go back to being friends—or brother-sister—that's okay with me." His words were flowing smoother now, and him relaxing made me relax a little, too.

"You don't think that would be too weird?"

"Weirder than this?"

I laughed, and instantly I felt lighter inside.

"Look, I know we didn't talk a lot before, but . . . maybe that could change, too."

He was being so open. So . . . reasonable. And in a flash of insight I saw that Brody Willow was the kind of guy you could actually build a life with.

But . . . what about the magic?

What about the crimson kissing?

I shook off the flurry of thoughts and said, "I'd like that." Then I added, "Your sister's not talking to me at all, you know. I've been trying to apologize to her, but she won't listen."

"Don't worry about Adrienne. I'll get her to read your note."
Then he muttered, "She needs to get off her high horse."

My immediate reaction was *That's right,* but with another wave of clarity it struck me that Adrienne had only been on her high horse for two days.

I'd been on mine for half a year.

90

Treasures and Trash

WHEN I WAS A LITTLE GIRL (and, okay, also when I was a not-so-little girl), my mother would put me in my room and tell me I was not to come out until it was tidy. She would close the door tightly behind her, and I would look around at the enormous mess that had piled up, not knowing where to begin.

An hour later she would look in and discover that I was reading a book. "Evangeline!" she would scold. "You haven't done a thing to clean up this mess!" She would then heave a big sigh and say, "Sort out the clothes. Put away the ones that aren't dirty, make a pile of the ones that are."

Off she'd go again, and because it's much simpler to have your mother wash, dry, fold, and put away your clothes than it is to sort them and put away the clean ones, I'd make a giant pile of all the clothes and get back to reading my book.

"These were all dirty? Really?" she'd ask, but then she'd focus on the next phase. "Now pick up all your papers. Go through them; decide what you want to keep and what you want to throw away."

Step by step she'd walk me through the process of tidying my room until we'd be down to a heap that neither of us quite knew what to do with. "Well," she'd finally say, "it won't go away on its own."

So we'd tackle the final heap. And some of the things that I'd elect to throw away she (in moments of sentimental weakness) would fish back out of the trash sack, finding remote places for them in my room.

Other things she'd be desperate to get rid of but I'd tug-o'-war for, saying how I would never-ever-ever in a million years part with it.

I'm better now at sorting, cleaning, folding, and putting away. What I have yet to conquer, however, is what to do with the final heap. How do you sort the treasure from the trash? When does something move from sentimental to disposable? And if you think you are ready to part with it, are you really? If you throw it away today, will you regret it tomorrow? Or will it be something you never think about again?

Sitting in my room after Brody's phone call, I realized that I *had* made significant progress in sorting out my messy life. I had *not* escaped to the pages of a book. I'd taken action. I'd analyzed and scrutinized and apologized.

But as much progress as I'd made, I was still left with a heap in the middle.

A heap I really didn't want to face.

A heap I really didn't know what to *do* with.

A heap known as my dad.

91

Opening the Sack

THE HEAP WASN'T GOING TO GO AWAY ON ITS OWN.

I knew that.

And although I'd stuffed it in the trash sack many times, Mom had fished it back out. It was like a favorite toy that had been shattered. I wanted it out of my sight so I could forget about it; she wanted to superglue it back together.

But the cracks always show when you superglue. And superglue doesn't work on everything. Try all you want, some things will not hold together (although your fingertips will be cemented for hours).

My dad was obviously the sort of thing that could not be superglued. So in my mind I'd stuffed him in a sack and hauled him out to the garage. And every time my mom opened the sack to take a sentimental peek at him, I refused to look. I yanked the drawstrings closed, waiting for the next trash pickup, when I might convince her to help me lift him into the bin and be done with him.

But it had been clear for some time now that she didn't want to be done with him.

So now here I was, taking a deep breath, peeking inside the sack and feeling the sentimental *Ohhhh*. The songs he'd sung for me, the concerts he'd taken me to, the stories he'd read to me, the bedtime tuck-ins, and the breakfast pancakes shaped like music notes and guitars . . . it all flooded across my heart.

And I let it.

Was it just the passage of time taking some of the sting away?

Was I tired of using the hurt he'd caused as a fuel?

Was Adrienne's unwillingness to listen or forgive making me see myself more clearly?

Perhaps it was a combination, but I finally caved in to the *Ohhhh*. I picked up the phone, sat down at the kitchen table, and dialed my old house's number.

"Hi, Dad," I managed when he answered the phone.

"Evangeline?" he asked, his voice soft, hopeful.

My throat pinched, my chin quivered, and then the strangest thing blurted out of my mouth. "Do you have any ice cream?"

92

Crossroads

My mom dropped her keys and her jaw when she eased through the door after work. "Better hurry," my dad said, tapping the side of the ice cream carton with his spoon.

I nodded, inspecting the mound on my spoon. "It's fudge-mocha swirl, and it's divine . . . and almost gone!"

My mom approached us cautiously but was smart enough not to make a fuss. Instead, she got herself a bowl and a spoon and pulled up a chair. "There's nothing I like better than an after-work ice cream party."

"How'd it go?" my dad asked, just like he used to. Just like the past half year hadn't happened.

But it had happened, and it was weird, and despite the fact that I'd spent an hour listening to my dad's heartfelt apologies and promises about the future, it didn't erase the past. Maybe it had been a crossroads for him. Maybe he had made a foolish turn when he should have gone straight. That didn't mean I could act like nothing had happened.

All of a sudden I was exhausted. All of a sudden I just wanted to go to bed.

My mom read my mood and held me by the arm as I started to stand. "I know tomorrow's *your* birthday, but this was the best present you could have given me."

I nodded once and said, "We're still a mess. Don't think we're not." I turned to my dad. "And just because every one of those guitar gods you love covered 'Crossroads,' don't forget what happened to the guy who wrote it."

My dad cringed, and my mom asked, "That was Eric Clapton, right? What happened to him?"

"It was Robert Johnson," my dad said. "And he was poisoned to death for womanizing."

I couldn't help grinning at him as I headed to my room. "You got off easy!"

93

The Key

THE NEXT MORNING I staggered into the kitchen to down a bowl of cold cereal, only to find my mother making my favorite (but rarely consumed) breakfast: scrambled eggs, sausage, and flaky butter-milk biscuits. "Happy birthday, angel!" she said with a dramatic wave of the spatula.

I looked around suspiciously for my dad.

I was just not ready to wake up to his presence.

Then I noticed that there were only two place settings. "Smells great," I said, sitting at the one with two little gold-wrapped boxes.

"You might want to wait until after breakfast to open those," she said, bringing a platter of food to the table.

"I might not!" I laughed. So I opened the top box and discovered a gold necklace with a heart-shaped pendant.

"Those are little rubies," she said, pointing out the tiny stones along one side of the heart.

I admired it, then draped the necklace back into the box. "It's very pretty, Mom. Thank you."

I started ripping into the second box, but as my mother scooped some eggs onto my plate, she said, "I'm serious about waiting until after you eat to open that one."

Immediately I understood why. "It's from Dad?"

She put a biscuit and sausage on my plate and gave a little shrug. "He wanted to be here, but I didn't think you were ready for that." She eyed the box. "And I really don't know how you're going to react to *that*."

So I nibbled on my breakfast, keeping one eye on the half-opened box.

What could it be?

Was it jewelry?

What else could fit in a box like that?

I shook it, and it rattled.

Was it . . . a *key*?

Had he finally bought me a *car*?

I found myself getting really upset. I didn't want him to buy me a car! Not like this! It would seem like a bribe. It would be just . . . wrong.

"Oh, just open it," my mom finally said. "You're not eating anyway!"

So I did. And what I discovered inside was, in fact, a key.

Only it wasn't a car key. It was tarnished and cheap-looking. Bigger than a luggage key but way smaller than a house key.

"What does *this* go to? Some kind of locker?"

Mom took in a deep breath. "You could say that."

I stared at her. "You're not going to make me guess, are you?"

She shook her head. "It's under my bed."

94

Under the Bed

THE LAST TIME I'D LOOKED UNDER MY MOTHER'S BED, I'd discovered *A Crimson Kiss*. It was like the place where this all began. Had she thought about that?

Probably not, but I couldn't help pausing for a moment.

What was under there now?

When I finally looked, I discovered that instead of books, there was now a long, flat, tattered rectangular case.

I knew right away what it was.

I gasped, then pulled it out by the handle and just stared.

"How do you feel about that?" my mother asked from the bedroom doorway.

There was a huge lump in my throat. "Strange," I choked out. I looked up at her. "You must've told him what I said about not teaching me."

"Oh, yeah," she said with a little smile. "Izzy had quite a talk with him, too."

"Izzy is in on this?"

She laughed. "Open it, would you?"

So I clicked open the latches and came face to frets with the Fender I'd played at Izzy's.

I covered my mouth. I stared. I giggled. And when I finally pulled it up by the neck, my hands were shaking.

It had a beautiful new padded black strap attached, and when I stood up and slung it over my shoulder, it didn't feel nearly as heavy.

It felt like it belonged.

Mom was shaking her head a little, tsking, as she leaned against the doorframe. "Oh, you do look good in guitar," she chuckled. Then she added, "Your dad says we've got to get you an amp, a tuner, some cables. . . ."

"Can we do that today?"

She straightened up. "You're talking about playing hooky?"

"Why not? It's my birthday!"

"No! You're going to school. You're going to college! You can love music, you can love your guitar, but you're *not* following in your father's footsteps!" Then softly she added, "But maybe you can call him and tell him you like it?"

I smiled at her and nodded.

I had no problem with that.

95

Give 'n' Take

MY DAD AND I HAD A REALLY GOOD TALK that morning, and although Mom offered me a ride to school, I knew she was really dying to go back to bed, so I told her I felt like walking. But when I left the condo, I discovered a familiar red truck parked along the curb.

Brody was leaning against the cab, waiting for me. "Happy birthday," he said with a shy smile. "I thought you might like a ride to school. Maybe let me buy you a frappuccino on the way?"

I laughed. "I can't believe you remembered!"

He opened the passenger door, and as I ducked in, I gasped. The upholstery had been completely redone. In place of the tattered black vinyl seats, there was now red and white diamond-tuft leather upholstery.

"Wow, wow, wow!" I said, sliding in. And when Brody took his seat behind the wheel, it struck me that he had been rotating through the same faded T-shirts all year, but that now, suddenly, he'd been able to completely redress his truck.

And that there wasn't actually anything "sudden" about it.

It had taken thought.

Planning.

Saving.

No . . . *investing.*

Brody was blushing. "So you like it?"

"It's *amazing.*" But as he started the truck, I felt all the open space in the cab and realized that someone was missing. "So . . . how's Adrienne getting to school?"

It was probably a somewhat thoughtless thing to ask, but Brody took it in stride. "She's getting a ride from Mom this morning."

"Ah," I said with a nod.

"I tried to talk to her about you, but she's still high on her horse, sorry."

"Thanks for trying," I said.

"So what did your parents get you for your birthday, do you know?"

"An electric guitar!" I said, practically bouncing up and down. "A Fender Strat. It's used, but it's *so* cool. It's . . . it's amazing!"

He studied me a moment. "An electric guitar." He pulled into traffic, murmuring, "That's a perfect present for you." Then he smiled at me and said, "To me you *are* music, you know?"

I blinked at him.

In all the pages of *A Crimson Kiss,* in all the movies I'd seen, all the stories I'd read, there was no line that compared.

96
Room 212

I REALLY DIDN'T WANT TO BE AT SCHOOL. I didn't want to be reminded of the damage I'd done to my "reputation." I didn't want to face the tests I'd bombed or the homework I hadn't done. And I especially didn't want to face being shut down by Adrienne.

What I wanted was to be home with my guitar.

Or suspended like Brody.

Anywhere but school.

But as I trudged over to first period, the thought of Robbie Marshall made me feel a little lighter. I owed him an apology way bigger than the one I'd given him for our kissing fiasco. I'd never once thought that his change from smart boy to dumb jock could be anything more than the alluring pull of jockdom and popularity, and I felt bad for stereotyping him like I had.

I was also impressed that he'd been willing to talk things out with me (despite some pretty erratic behavior on my part).

So when he caught up to me outside of math and flashed his diamond-dusted smile and said, "Hey! Can you tutor me today?" my mind kind of blanked on the fact that it was my birthday and that there was a guitar waiting for me at home. I just said, "Sure!" and told him to meet me in Room 212 after school.

After that, I had a surprisingly calm and focused day. At lunch I ate in the usual spot in case Adrienne decided she wanted to forgive me on my birthday, but apparently she did not.

I tried not to let it get to me too much, and after school I went straight to Room 212.

"You're back?" Mrs. Huffington asked, obviously surprised to see me.

"I'm meeting a friend here to tutor him in math."

She fluttered uncomfortably, glancing at Lisa and the other two tutors. "I see."

Obviously I was violating some tutoring protocol, so I said, "Look. I'll help anyone, as long as they don't stink and aren't rude. If you're not comfortable talking to Roper about his odor, how do you expect me to be comfortable tutoring him?"

"Amen," Lisa muttered.

Then Robbie walked in.

"Hey," he said, giving me his gorgeous smile.

"*This* is who you're tutoring?" Mrs. Huffington asked.

I made the introductions and said, "Robbie is lost in a deep, dark mathematic abyss, and I'm going to help him find his way out."

"I see . . . ," Mrs. Huffington said, but judging by the look in her eye, she was seeing more than was there.

Robbie, though, was amazing. He didn't flirt, he didn't fidget, he focused. And he must've noticed how Lisa and another female tutor were ogling him, but he didn't let it interrupt his concentration. He asked questions, he worked problems, and he kept at it until everyone else was long gone. Mrs. Huffington finally shooed us out, saying, "You'll have to resume this on Tuesday, or elsewhere. It's time for me to be getting home."

"Feel better?" I asked Robbie as we walked toward the parking lot.

"Tons." Then he turned to me and said, "You're a really good teacher."

I smiled at him. "So you want to meet again on Tuesday?"

He smiled back. "Absolutely."

He offered me a ride home, but I decided it would be wiser to walk.

Besides, there was someplace I wanted to go on the way home.

And I wanted to do it alone.

97

Good Lighting

"BUBBLES!" IZZY SAID when I stepped inside Groove Records. He was smiling from ear to ear.

"You are such a sneak!" I laughed, running up to hug him.

"Happy birthday, kiddo," he said, hugging me back. Then he laughed and said, "Your old man has terrible timing!"

"So it wasn't just that the guitar was gone?"

"No! He was hiding right here!" he said, pointing behind a bargain bin of CDs. "I was sweating bullets."

"Well, you fooled me! And I'm dying to get home to play it."

He seemed shocked. "You've got a Fender Strat at home and you went to *school* today?"

I laughed. "You're a bad influence!"

He chuckled. "I know, I know." Then he hurried back behind the counter. "Here. Take this. You need something until you get a real amp."

He handed over a guitar cable and a small greenish plastic thing about the size of a bar of soap. "It's called a Smokey. Just plug in and play. It may not be a Marshall, but you'll have fun."

I hugged him again, then ran all the way home.

I couldn't wait to try out my guitar, but when I caught a glimpse of myself as I passed by the entry mirror, I hesitated, then moved back for a second look.

I'd stopped wearing makeup days ago, but I didn't feel plain-Jane or washed out. My cheeks were rosy, my eyes seemed clear and bright, and my haircut and highlights still looked great.

Maybe it was the lighting, the afternoon sun coming through the glass arch of the front door at just the right angle.

Or maybe, I thought as I smiled at my reflection, I was just starting to feel good in my own skin.

98

Shelved

AT LONG LAST, *Grayson held her in his arms and gazed upon her radiant beauty. How had nature managed such exquisite perfection? Soft as a dove, with eyes pure as crystals, she was like a pool of sunshine, a cleansing rain to his soul.*

As Delilah searched Grayson's deep, rich eyes, she saw an uncommon tenderness, a caring beyond earthly confines, a depth to his heart only dreams could imagine. With a small, helpless gasp, she surrendered to the strength of his arms, relaxing in their loving bondage, knowing he would never let her fall.

As his lips descended, she could feel the pulsing of his heart, could taste the heat of his

desire. In that moment, she forgot the world, for-
got Elise, forgot the pain that had engulfed her
for so long, and embraced his hunger with the
sweet, unbridled abandon of her soul.

I read the passage one last time, and then, with a heavy sigh, I filed *A Crimson Kiss* alongside *Lord of the Rings* and *The Princess Bride* on my makeshift stacked-crate bookcase.

In the week I'd had it, my guitar had edged out *A Crimson Kiss*. Where the story was something I could imagine, the guitar was tangible; something I could hold.

But still. A guitar cannot deliver a crimson kiss. And although the book might have lost its effect on me after so many readings, by shelving it I felt like I was also shelving my fantasy.

Maybe there really was no such thing as the perfect kiss.

Maybe it was just as Adrienne had said.

Simply fiction.

And I did need to deal with reality.

I'd been trying all week to patch things up with Adrienne. I'd waited outside her classrooms. I'd waited outside the Performance Pavilion. I'd called her and left messages. I'd written her notes and explained how my kiss with Paxton was not really a kiss at all but merely a collision of lips followed by a shove-off. But none of it seemed to matter to her. She continued to ditch me, dis me, or simply ignore me.

I didn't want to give up, but I didn't really know what else to do. By the end of the week I was wondering if lifelong friendships were like perfect kisses.

Maybe they didn't really exist.

But on Friday night (after doing scales on my guitar until my fingers were almost bleeding) I made a fateful decision.

It was the opening night of Adrienne's spring choral performance.

I was going to attend.

99

Yodeling the Night Away

ONLY A REAL FRIEND (or duty-bound relative) would attend a Larkmont High choral performance. Putting it as kindly as possible,
they're sad. The singing is good, but the songs are always strange,
never-before-heard numbers that were most likely rescued from
the depths of a waste bin by an overzealous janitor more than a
hundred years ago. (I'm just speculating, of course, but I can't seem
to come up with any other explanation for the sorry song selec-
tions.)

To make matters worse, the choir is . . . sparse. There are *maybe*
five singers on each part. And because it's a tradition (or something), they stagger the singers on three-tier aluminum risers across
the entire Performance Pavilion stage. Mrs. Vogel plays the baby
grand on one end, Mr. Vogel conducts from in front, but no amount
of gesticulating on his part (or hers) can conceal the fact that there
are about twenty singers on risers that could comfortably hold
a hundred.

Anyway, I picked up a small rose bouquet for Adrienne on my way to the Pavilion, then got my ticket at the box office, accepted a Xeroxed program from an usher, and went inside.

The saving grace of any Larkmont choral production is the Performance Pavilion itself. It's new and plush, has stadium and balcony seating, and belongs nowhere near Larkmont High School. It *is* on campus but on the outskirts, and I don't believe the school actually *owns* it. I think the money was donated by an outside source and is maintained by some foundation.

Why else would the box office workers, the concession people, the ushers, and the security guards all be senior citizens?

If I'd been there to get extra credit for some class (as Miss Ryder has been known to offer for dramatic performances), I would have chosen a seat in the back or up in the balcony. But I was there to get friendship credit, and for that I needed to be visible. And although there were only a few minutes remaining until showtime, seating was still wide open. So after looking around for any other Willows who might be in the audience (and finding none), I chose a seat right up front and got comfy.

"Welcome to the Performance Pavilion!" came a recorded voice over the loudspeaker. "Please quiet your cell phone, and remember: Food, drink, and gum are not permitted inside the theater. Also, for the performers' safety, do not use flash photography. Please take your seat, as the performance is about to begin!"

All twenty-five audience members got ready.

The curtain parted.

Mrs. Vogel started tinkling the keys of the baby grand, Mr. Vogel's hands went into action, and the choir was off, putting their heart and soul into janitorial pilferage selection number one: "How Mightily the River Doth Flow."

The girls were all wearing blue taffeta gowns, and Adrienne looked absolutely gorgeous. Her hair was pulled back in an updo, with little ringlets falling from her temples, in front of her ears, and at the nape of her neck. Her diamond pendant sparkled under the lights.

I soaked her in, remembering how we had climbed into her attic as third graders and discovered boxes of her mother's old clothes. Funky, oversized sweaters, dresses with wide belts and padded shoulders, shoes with radical heels, and the jackpot of dress-up: a box labeled Bridesmaid Dresses. (Mrs. Willow had, we learned later, been a bridesmaid eight times before becoming a bride.)

The blue taffeta gown Adrienne was now wearing reminded me very much of one of those bridesmaid dresses. It was strange to see her looking so grown up, and yet still see her in my mind's eye, up in the attic, playing dress-up.

It also drifted through my mind that in a way *I'd* been playing dress-up. I'd borrowed my mother's clothes, her makeup, her perfume...

I wondered when the final shift into adulthood happened. When did you go from playing grown-up to *being* grown up? Sometimes it seemed like my parents were still playing at being grown-ups. Seventeen years after having a kid, they didn't seem completely comfortable in grown-up clothes.

This is how I whiled away the time through "The Trumpet Vine on Window Nigh," and "Roses Blue and Cold," and "Underneath the Pock'd Moon." Then Mrs. Vogel announced the Germanic origins of the next tune, and when the choir launched into "Ach Du Lieber Meinen Hund," my attention turned to Paxton.

That boy is very serious about his singing.

A little too serious.

But between songs I noticed that *his* attention turned to a certain girl in blue taffeta. (Well, okay, all the girls were in blue taffeta, but I'm talking about Adrienne here.) He was a riser behind her and a section over, with only two singers between them. (In other words, he was a mile away.) But because the risers were arranged in a shallow U shape, he could see her beautiful updo (and part of her profile) with a simple twist of his bow-tied neck.

And twist he did!

This made me inexplicably happy. I was dying to pull Adrienne aside and tell her. Dying to give her all the nitty-gritty details of the focus of his attentions. Dying to watch her jump up and down in giddy bliss.

Maybe none of this was news to her (she had, after all, gotten at least one ride from the guy). But maybe it was!

Suddenly it was like there was nothing weird between us. We were back in the attic, the best of friends, and I just wanted to deliver the news!

When the last song before intermission ("Yodeling the Day Away") was finally over, I knew I couldn't wait through the second half of the program.

I had to go backstage.

Now!

100

Witness

My attempt at going backstage was thwarted by an eighty-year-old security guard wielding a bad attitude.

"I said no, miss," he snarled after my third attempt at talking my way past him. "You do understand the definition of No, don't you?"

I frowned at him.

Smartass.

So I took my flowers and went outside. I knew my way around! I knew about the back doors! I didn't need some old guy blocking me from delivering some very exciting news!

The night air felt great, and I inhaled deeply as I walked toward the back of the building. I could smell the pine trees that lined the property. It was a sweet and comforting fragrance. Adrienne wouldn't stay mad at me forever! She couldn't!

I turned the corner full throttle, but then immediately stopped short and hugged the wall. Paxton had Adrienne by the hand and was pulling her outside through the back door that I'd been heading toward. She was laughing and he was smiling, and the moment the door closed, he swept her around to face him.

A security light glowed like a moon high above them. It washed them in a warm softness, wrapping them in a moment that was all theirs. And as they gazed into each other's eyes, *my* heart began to race.

He was going to kiss her!

I both wanted to disappear and move closer. So (very sensibly) I stayed put, pressing harder against the wall.

And then, like the scene from the book come to life, I watched Adrienne search Paxton's eyes; I watched him drink in her beauty. As he pulled her toward him, I saw her melt in his arms.

When he kissed her, I could see that the world fell away around them, I could feel their happiness radiate out through the night.

My knees gave way and I slid down the wall.

Now *that* was a crimson kiss.

101

In the Powder Room

LONG AFTER PAXTON AND ADRIENNE had gone back inside, I sat outside in the dark, stunned. Here I'd been the one chasing down a crimson kiss, and somehow *Adrienne* had found one.

How had this happened?

Finally I got up, dusted off, and slipped through the back door. The second portion of the program was well under way, so I waited in the ladies' powder room, which is like a chorus line dressing room. In addition to an alcove of pearlized toilets, there are lots of mirrors, lots of vanity lights, benches, and long racks to hang clothes.

While I waited for the second act to be over, I spent time scrutinizing myself in the mirror.

Paxton had turned out to be a crimson kisser.

But not with me.

So *was* it me? Were all those unsatisfying kisses *my* fault?

Was it my approach?

My expectations?

I'd been looking for a crimson kiss, but I hadn't invested emotionally in any of the guys. I'd just expected the fantasy and the moment and the desire for a crimson kiss to make it happen.

And what had I ended up with?

A bunch of junky kisses.

When the show was over and Adrienne came into the powder room, the only thing she seemed able to do was stare at me.

So I grabbed her wrist, yanked her over to a bench, pressed the flowers on her, and whispered, "I saw Paxton kiss you!"

Her eyes came to life, her face beamed with an angelic glow, and her wall of silence crumbled. "You did?" she asked, grabbing my forearms.

I nodded. "It was the most amazing thing I have ever seen." I leaned in. "That was a real-life crimson kiss!"

"It was, wasn't it?" she gasped. "Oh, my God, Evangeline, I thought I was going to faint!"

I smiled at her. "I could tell."

"Where *were* you?"

I shrugged. "Coming around the building so I could sneak in the back door and see you. I wanted to tell you how he kept looking at you during the first act."

"He did?"

I laughed, because it was such a cute thing for her to wonder. "Come on! Like you're surprised? He *kissed* you!"

She giggled, then looked at me and suddenly burst into tears. "Oh, Evangeline!"

My eyes spilled over as we fell into a hug. "I have missed you so much!"

"I've missed you so much, too!" she said.

I pulled away and sniffed. "Oh, right!"

"I'm serious! I really have!"

I nodded. "Me too."

She grabbed me by the arms again. "Can you come over? Spend the night? We've got so much catching up to do!"

I smiled and nodded. "Sounds perfect."

102

Investments

It's been a month since I witnessed Adrienne and Paxton's crimson kiss. It was not their one and only, either. Adrienne reports there have been many more, and I see no end in sight for those lovebirds.

I'm actually very happy for her.

Okay, a little jealous, but happy.

I, on the other hand, have gone into kissing remission. Not that I haven't been tempted, especially since I've had some pretty good offers (most notably from gorgeous Lars Wilson, who, like Stu, claims to be in possession of a crimson kiss).

That may be, but for now I'm resisting the urge to find out.

Instead, I've been doing something a short tier down from crimson kissing.

Shopping!

It started because Adrienne is going to the prom with Paxton (who I finally got to apologize to), so she and I spent a full week scouring stores for a perfect fairy-tale dress. But while we were looking for her, we also stumbled across some cool things for me. No dresses—just simple, casual clothes somewhere between my mom's wardrobe and my old frumpy T's. Things that feel like me. My favorite is a white T-shirt (with cap sleeves and a scoop neck, of course). There are no words or brand logos, just six vertical rifles lined up beside one purple guitar. It's a think-about-it shirt, and I like that.

I also (in a completely different way) like the dress Adrienne chose. It's a full-length deep red Empire-waist gown with pretty faux-jewel detailing on the straps and bodice. She looks *gorgeous* in it, and when I get done with her hair and makeup, Paxton will fall to one knee and swear his eternal love.

I might be jealous about that, too, but I'm not. I feel like I'm just now figuring myself out, and I need to give that a little time before including somebody else.

So instead of thinking about kissing or boyfriends, I'm investing.

In my guitar playing, in my schoolwork, in my friendship with Adrienne, and in my family.

Mom, Dad, and I have been to four counseling sessions now, and Dad and I have also had some good guitar sessions. He's taking the father-daughter thing slow and easy, which has helped. And music has always been something we could talk about.

I've also been investing (to my own surprise) in Robbie Marshall.

After completing my community service hours by tutoring Robbie in Room 212, we moved the math-help sessions to Starbucks. We don't just hang out, either. We do homework, and he's serious about it. It's a standing date twice a week, one I really look forward to. Robbie is actually very funny, and his math grade is now up to a B−, which makes me proud. I just don't know if I'm brave enough to ever kiss him again. (Although, it has crossed my mind that if the math tutoring has gone this well, then maybe he'd be a quick-study kisser, too.)

The best thing about Robbie is that when I turned him down for prom, he just smiled and said, "So maybe we'll go next year," and then didn't ask anyone else out.

So maybe he's investing in me, too.

But besides getting to know Robbie, I've also been getting to know Brody better. Each of them is aware of the other, so it's not like I'm going behind anyone's back. And now that Mom's given notice at the condo and we're slowly moving things back to the house, I use the computer to e-mail Brody a *lot*. We mostly discuss books and music and politics. It seems a little silly to e-mail when we're right down the street from each other, but I was practically part of his family for years, and this is how I'm finally getting to know what he thinks (and that boy thinks *deep*).

In a few months, Brody'll be going to live in Connecticut, but I think we'll still e-mail each other like we do now. I hope we will anyway.

So even though there were shocking and embarrassing (and *slobbery*) moments, I learned a lot from my spree as a serial kisser. I understand myself better, my parents better . . . I understand that forgiveness may be hard, but it's a liberating first step forward . . . and I understand that there's real healing power in the delivery of an apology.

And in a Fender Strat plugged into a Marshall amp!

I also finally see that a crimson kiss isn't something you can chase, because it's more than just the passionate meeting of mouths.

It's a confession.

It's the truth your lips whisper to someone you love.

Don't miss these other terrific novels from Wendelin Van Draanen

Wendelin Van Draanen

FLIPPED

New bonus material inside!

"We flipped over this fantastic book, its gutsy girl Juli and its wise, wonderful ending."
—*Chicago Tribune*

FROM THE AUTHOR OF *FLIPPED*
Wendelin Van Draanen

RUNAWAY

"Will grab readers from the first entry."
—*The Sacramento Bee*

FROM THE AUTHOR OF *FLIPPED*
Wendelin Van Draanen

The Running Dream

"Jessica's determination and passion will touch everyone who reads this story."
—*The Examiner*